Hi, I'm JIMMY!
Like me, you probably noticed the world is run by adults.
But ask yourself: Who would do the best job
of making books that *kids* will love?
Yeah. **Kids!**

So that's how the idea of JIMMY books came to life.
We want every JIMMY book to be so good
that when you're finished, you'll say,
"PLEASE GIVE ME ANOTHER BOOK!"

Give this one a try and see if you agree.
(If not, you're probably an adult!)

JIMMY PATTERSON BOOKS FOR YOUNG READERS

JAMES PATTERSON PRESENTS

How to Be a Supervillain by Michael Fry
How to Be a Supervillain: Born to Be Good by Michael Fry
How to Be a Supervillain: Bad Guys Finish First by Michael Fry
Sci-Fi Junior High by John Martin and Scott Seegert
Sci-Fi Junior High: Crash Landing by John Martin and Scott Seegert
The Unflushables by Ron Bates
Ernestine, Catastrophe Queen by Merrill Wyatt
Scouts by Shannon Greenland

THE MIDDLE SCHOOL SERIES BY JAMES PATTERSON

Middle School, The Worst Years of My Life
Middle School: Get Me Out of Here!
Middle School: Big Fat Liar
Middle School: How I Survived Bullies, Broccoli, and Snake Hill
Middle School: Ultimate Showdown
Middle School: Save Rafe!
Middle School: Just My Rotten Luck
Middle School: Dog's Best Friend
Middle School: Escape to Australia
Middle School: From Zero to Hero
Middle School: Born to Rock

THE I FUNNY SERIES BY JAMES PATTERSON

I Funny
I Even Funnier
I Totally Funniest
I Funny TV
I Funny: School of Laughs
The Nerdiest, Wimpiest, Dorkiest I Funny Ever

THE TREASURE HUNTERS SERIES BY JAMES PATTERSON

Treasure Hunters
Treasure Hunters: Danger Down the Nile
Treasure Hunters: Secret of the Forbidden City
Treasure Hunters: Peril at the Top of the World
Treasure Hunters: Quest for the City of Gold
Treasure Hunters: All-American Adventure

TREASURE HUNTERS

ALL-AMERICAN ADVENTURE

BY **JAMES PATTERSON**

AND **CHRIS GRABENSTEIN**

ILLUSTRATED BY
JULIANA NEUFELD

JIMMY PATTERSON BOOKS
LITTLE, BROWN AND COMPANY
NEW YORK BOSTON LONDON

Copyright © 2019 by James Patterson
Illustrations by Juliana Neufeld

JIMMY Patterson Books / Little, Brown and Company
Hachette Book Group
1290 Avenue of the Americas, New York, NY 10104
JimmyPatterson.org

First Edition: June 2019

JIMMY Patterson Books is an imprint of Little, Brown and Company, a division of Hachette Book Group, Inc. The Little, Brown name and logo are trademarks of Hachette Book Group, Inc. The JIMMY Patterson Books® name and logo are trademarks of JBP Business, LLC.

The publisher is not responsible for websites (or their content) that are not owned by the publisher.

The Hachette Speakers Bureau provides a wide range of authors for speaking events. To find out more, go to hachettespeakersbureau.com or call (866) 376-6591.

ISBN 978-0-316-41743-3

Library of Congress Cataloging-in-Publication Data
Names: Patterson, James, 1947– author. | Grabenstein, Chris, author. | Neufeld, Juliana, 1982– illustrator.
Title: All-American adventure / James Patterson and Chris Grabenstein ; illustrated by Juliana Neufeld.
Description: First edition. | New York : Little, Brown and Company, 2019. | Series: Treasure hunters; book 6 | Summary: When they uncover a conspiracy against America and its fundamental freedoms, the Kidd children, accompanied by their great uncle, crisscross the country in a race to prove that a newly-discovered copy of the Bill of Rights is a forgery.
Identifiers: LCCN 2019015797 | ISBN 978-0-316-41743-3 (alk. paper)
Subjects: | CYAC: Adventure and adventurers—Fiction. | Conspiracies—Fiction. | Counterfeits and counterfeiting—Fiction. | Buried treasure—Fiction. | Brothers and sisters—Fiction. | Twins—Fiction.
Classification: LCC PZ7.P27653 Al 2019 | DDC [Fic]—dc23
LC record available at https://lccn.loc.gov/2019015797

10 9 8 7 6 5 4 3 2 1

LSC-C

Printed in the United States of America

This one is for Teddy Penn—
a great reader with a big
imagination with a shiny-star
future.
—James Patterson

QUICK NOTE FROM BICK KIDD

G ot to make this super speedy, guys.

Half an hour ago, we were bored out of our minds. Now? We're finally on an adventure—one with a time limit, too!

Once again, I, Bickford "Bick" Kidd, will be the one telling this tale. My twin sister, Rebecca "Beck" Kidd, will be handling the illustrations.

But she better scribble fast.

Like I said, we're on an adventure!

PART I
FAMILY TREASURES

CHAPTER 1

There was an elephant lurking in the shadows behind us.

It just stood there. Stiff and silent. I figured he was waiting for us to make one false move and then—*boink!*—pointy tusk to the butt.

"Um, can we get out of here?" whispered Beck.

"Chya," said our big brother, Tailspin Tommy. "That elephant has its trunk curled up like it just sniffed a bag of hot roasted peanuts."

Definitely not the first thing I'd think to experience in a museum—but stranger things have happened to us Kidds.

"Or, he just got a whiff of Bick," added Beck.
"He smells like hot roasted gym socks."

"Do not," I countered.

"Do, too."

"You guys?" whispered Storm, our brainy older
sister. "We have only fifteen more minutes to find
the Hope Diamond!"

Ah, the Hope Diamond. The treasure we were
currently hunting. It's got 45.52 carats (the kind

they use to measure diamonds, not the kind bunnies nibble). It's also 45.52 times bigger than the average engagement ring, which, Storm told us (because she memorizes trivial factoids in her spare time), is only about *one* carat. That's right. The Hope is also the Humongous. It's about the size of a walnut and is the largest deep-blue diamond in the world. Some people say it's worth a quarter of a billion dollars!

They also say it's cursed.

"It was originally plucked out of the brow of an Indian temple statue by a Hindu priest," Storm had told us the night before we set off on our adventure.

"The priest's punishment for the unholy theft was a slow and agonizing death. The diamond showed up in Europe in 1642 when a greedy merchant sold it to King Louis XIV for a handsome profit. But the merchant didn't get to spend his money because he was soon mauled to death by a pack of wild dogs."

Storm. She loves the gory details. Says they make history way more interesting.

Anyway, she told us that when Marie Antoinette (Queen "Let Them Eat Cake") owned it, she was caught trying to flee France with the ginormous diamond. That was in 1791, during the French Revolution, so the big blue bauble was seized by the French revolutionary government.

"They also chopped off Marie Antoinette's head, so she probably didn't need a diamond necklace anymore," Storm had added.

The Hope Diamond was then stolen. More people bought and sold it (many of them getting murdered or losing their fortunes along the way). Finally, an American heiress brought it to the United States. It's why we're on our current expedition in the heart of Washington, DC.

We're also trying to ignore the whole "Hope Diamond Curse" thing.

But it might've found us.

Because ten seconds after we slipped away from the scary elephant lurking in the dark, we were face-to-face with two snarling lions attacking a wildebeest!

CHAPTER 2

"**D**udes?" whispered Tommy. "Can we, like, lose all these angry mammals?" My knees are starting to get a little shaky.

I totally agreed with my big brother. Especially when I saw what looked like a tiger ready to leap off a cliff!

"Follow me," said Storm, backtracking to where we had spotted the elephant. "Up this way," she directed. She doesn't need a map because she has a photographic memory—the map was in her head.

Suddenly, I heard footfalls echoing in the distance.

"Somebody's following us!" I said as quietly as I could while running up a steep set of steps.

"They probably know about the Hope Diamond!" said Beck.

"Uh, everybody knows about it," countered Storm. "It's sort of famous."

"This way!" I said because I saw what I thought would be an excellent hiding place.

I was wrong.

I yanked open a series of doors and we were, somehow, transported to a tropical rain forest. We're talking 90 degrees with 90 percent humidity. A swarm of butterflies, some with ginormous wings, fluttered near our faces. One tickled my nose with its flappers.

"I have something tangled in my hair!" shrieked Beck.

"That's a Madagascar moon moth," said Storm, calmly. "And a Gulf fritillary butterfly. And, I believe, a pink cattleheart. Hard to tell, it's so dark in here."

"Because it's the middle of the night and we're not supposed to be here!" I exclaimed. "This is a top-secret treasure hunt!"

"Then you might want to lower your voice, little bro," suggested Tommy. "Maybe quit exclaiming stuff."

We heard a door swing open. Felt the whoosh

of air being sucked into the airlock chamber that we'd just passed through.

"They're following us!" I said.

"Out the back door," said Beck, pointing straight ahead. There was a butterfly perched on her fingertip. One that looked like it had an owl face printed on its wings.

We dashed through one door, stepped into a room with a major fan stirring up a breeze, made sure that no moths or butterflies were hitching a ride on our clothes or in our hair, and then yanked open an exit.

Ten feet later, we were surrounded by bugs. We're talking tarantulas, praying mantises, bees—the works. It was like every creepy crawler in the world was there, waiting for us in the dark.

"This place bugs me!" I shouted as quietly as I could because whoever was chasing us was right behind us, coming out of that second door from butterfly world.

"This way!" whispered Storm.

She led us into a chamber filled with mummies and then one lined with bones.

"We only have two more minutes!" We're not going to make it!

We rounded a corner, passed a gift shop, and headed into a dimly lit room filled with sparkling glass cases.

There it was. Sitting in a display case under its own mini rotunda. The Hope Diamond!

"Well done, children," said Dad, stepping out of the shadows, clicking his stopwatch.

"You made it up here with time to spare," added Mom, who'd been hiding in the rare gems room with Dad.

"You guys?" I said.

"Yes, Bick?"

"I don't want to sound ungrateful, but—"

"This was the easiest, lamest, most boring, worst make-believe treasure hunt ever!" said Beck, finishing my thought for me. It's a twin thing.

"I concur," said Storm. "All we really needed was a floor plan for the Smithsonian National Museum of Natural History."

"Chya," said Tommy, grabbing one from a nearby rack. "It's like printed right in here. See?" He started tapping icons. "First floor, Mammals. Second floor. Butterfly Pavilion, Live Insect Zoo, Mummies, Bones, Gift Shop, Hope Diamond. Even I could figure it out."

"But you had a time limit," said Mom, acting

as if that made the whole thing some kind of huge challenge.

It didn't.

But the security guards who barged into the room swinging their bulky flashlights?

They definitely made the whole adventure a little more interesting.

CHAPTER 3

"What's going on here?" asked one of the Smithsonian security guards.

"Just a little harmless family fun, George," said Dad, who obviously knew the guy.

"Oh, hi, Dr. Kidd," said George, holstering his flashlight. "Didn't see you there."

"Hi, Doc," said the other guard, waving his flashlight like a chunky baton.

"Good evening, Jayden."

"We hope we didn't cause you guys any trouble," added Mom.

"Nah, not at all," said Jayden, hiking up his belt a little. "Needed the exercise."

"Gets kind of boring around here at night," added George.

"Tell us about it," muttered Beck. She wasn't a big fan of fake treasure hunts inside museums. Me, neither.

But it was the best we could do for the time being. Mom and Dad had agreed to curate an exhibit at the Smithsonian about the Lost City of Paititi, which we had discovered deep in the rain forests of Peru, where it was even sweatier than inside that hot and humid Butterfly Pavilion.

"Can't wait for your exhibit to open," said George.

"Me, neither," said Jayden. "Will you be displaying any of the real gold?"

Dad shook his head. "No. That belongs to the people of Peru."

"But," said Mom, "we're putting together quite an exciting diorama."

"Chya," said Tommy. "Visitors can bust a dam and watch Paititi emerge from its lake, just like we saw."

"Cool," said Jayden.

"Totally," agreed Tommy.

Then they knocked knuckles.

"What goes on in here?" asked a grouchy man in a tweed jacket as he stepped into the Hope Diamond exhibit hall.

"Me and Jayden were fist bumping," replied Tommy. "It's a bro thing."

"Dr. Kidd?" The grumpy man arched an eyebrow. It was bushier than most mustaches. It kind of reminded me of a caterpillar from that Insect Zoo.

"Good evening, Professor Hingleburt," said Dad. "What brings you to the museum at this late hour?"

"My radio!" replied the angry professor, unclipping a walkie-talkie from his belt so he could wiggle-waggle it at everybody.

HARUMPH!

PROFESSOR HINGLEBURT. IF HE WAS ONE OF THE SEVEN DWARFS, HE'D DEFINITELY BE GRUMPY.

"I was next door, at the American History Museum. Heard we had intruders over here. I raced across the Victory Garden as quickly as I could."

In case you've never been to Washington, DC, the Smithsonian is a collection of several different museums mostly lined up between the Washington Monument and the United States Capitol Building.

SMITHSONIAN NATIONAL MUSEUMS

WE ARE HERE.
SO, UNFORTUNATELY,
IS PROFESSOR HINGLEBURT.

AFRICAN AMERICAN HISTORY AND CULTURE MUSEUM (FUTURE) SITE

WEST BUILDING   EAST BUILDING

AMERICAN HISTORY MUSEUM

NATURAL HISTORY MUSEUM

SCULPTURE GARDEN

NATIONAL GALLERY OF ART

THE NATIONAL MALL

WASHINGTON MONUMENT

RIPLEY CENTER

ARTS AND INDUSTRIES

SMITHSONIAN CASTLE

AMERICAN INDIAN MUSEUM

U.S. CAPITOL

FREER GALLERY

HAUPT GARDEN

HIRSHHORN MUSEUM

AIR AND SPACE MUSEUM

SACKLER GALLERY AFRICAN ART MUSEUM

WE'D LIKE TO SEND HIM OVER TO THE NATIONAL AIR AND SPACE MUSEUM. LAUNCH HIM TO THE MOON.

In addition to being crabby and cranky, Professor Hingleburt was also bald. His eyebrows were the hairiest thing on his head.

"I'm sorry we interrupted you, Professor," said Dad with an easy smile. "Were you doing research next door?"

"Indeed I was!" said Professor Hingleburt. "I am on the verge of announcing a major discovery of monumental historical significance."

"Is that so?" said Dad. "Congratulations."

"Therefore," said Professor Hingleburt, "as a serious scholar, I would appreciate it if you could keep your children on a tighter leash. We can't have them running amok wreaking havoc!"

"We apologize," said Mom.

"It was all in good fun," added Dad.

"And highly educational," I added. "Who knew there were butterflies that looked like owls?"

"The kids didn't break anything or, you know, let any tarantulas out of their cages," said George the guard.

"Gave us a real run for our money, though," added the other guard, Jayden, patting his belly.

"Almost made me burp. Had a double cheese-burger for dinner..."

"Well, Dr. and Mrs. Kidd," huffed Professor Hingleburt, "just because you're working here doesn't mean your children should be allowed to run around these hallowed halls at all hours."

"Mom's a doctor, too," said Storm.

"Then you both should know better!" said the pouting professor. "Too much freedom is a dangerous thing. It leads to anarchy and lawlessness!"

"But, Dr. Hingleburt," said Dad, "freedom is what America is all about. Life, liberty, and the pursuit of happiness."

"Is that so?" protested Dr. Hingleburt. "Well, maybe that's why this country's in such sad shape. With packs of wild children pursuing their happiness by charging willy-nilly through our cherished national treasures."

"The children won't do it again, Professor," said Dad. "I promise."

"There will be no more after-hours explorations in any more national landmarks," added Mom.

Beck and I looked at each other and sighed.

"There goes this weekend's race up the steps of the Washington Monument," she mumbled.

I nodded. "And that thing at the Lincoln Memorial."

It sounded like however long we were stuck in DC, we'd have to behave like ordinary kids instead of the wild things on a wild rumpus we were born to be.

We'd have to be bored out of our gourds, instead.

CHAPTER 4

The next day, we joined Mom and Dad in the sealed-off corner of the Smithsonian where they were setting up their exhibit about our time in Peru.

"Visitors will walk through this corridor and feel as if they've just entered the Amazon rain forest," Mom explained as the six of us traipsed through a maze of fake plants, all of them dripping with water.

"Whoa. How'd you get it to be so muggy in here?" asked Tommy, checking both his armpits for sweat rings.

"Dozens of humidifiers hidden behind the scenery," explained Dad.

"You might consider selling sweat bands at the gift shop," suggested Beck, wiping her brow. "Especially for when Bick visits."

We rounded a bend and came to a display of wax dummies depicting the nasty loggers we'd met on our last adventure. They looked like scurvy pirates with chain saws cutting down all the trees in the area illegally.

"Deforestation is, as you guys know, a major concern in tropical rain forests," said Mom.

"Indeed," spouted Storm. "In the Amazon, nearly seventeen percent of the trees have been chopped down in the last fifty years."

"Check it out!" I said, pointing to a pile of fake logs that seemed to be smoldering. "The smoke looks so real!"

"We wanted to demonstrate the slash and burn techniques being used by too many loggers," explained Dad. "We are striving to totally immerse our guests in that experience."

They were doing a good job. The room smelled like a wet bag of charcoal.

"Demonstrating the smoke is super-important," said Storm, jumping in. "NASA satellite reports suggest that the heavy smoke from Amazon forest fires inhibits cloud formation and, therefore, reduces rainfall. That means all this deforestation could change the Amazon rain forest into the Amazon no-rain/no-forest."

"Once our visitors complete their journey through the rain forest," said Mom, "they'll enter the main hall and see…this!"

"Whoa!" said Tommy (again) as we stepped into a wide-open circular space. "It's the volcano crater. The lake where we finally found the Lost City of Paititi. And there's the stone table where the bad guys almost, you know…"

Storm slid her finger across her chest in a slashing X. "Cut out your heart for an ancient Incan-style human sacrifice?"

"Yeah. That."

"We're going to skip that episode in our exhibit," said Dad. "Keep it rated PG."

Tommy nodded. "Smart move. Fer shure."

"We're still working on the mechanics to topple the dam and drain the water out of the lake," said Dad. "But here's what we have so far."

He went to a wall and bopped a flat red button.

"Whoa!" This time we all said it with Tommy.

Miniature boulders mechanically toppled away, opening floodgates. Gushing water sluiced out of the fake lake to reveal a miniature model of the shimmering gold city of Paititi that would've been right at home on a model train set. It looked just like the real thing, only eighty-seven times tinier.

"We'll be ready to open to the public in two—" Mom started. But she didn't get to finish that thought.

Because a fire alarm went off.

Sprinklers started twirling and spritzing in the ceiling.

That smoldering log pile? It must've been too realistic for the smoke detectors. Because all of a sudden, it was really raining inside Mom and Dad's fake rain forest.

CHAPTER 5

"We need to push back the opening date," Mom told us over dinner that night in our short-term DC rental apartment.

"We also need to rethink the whole 'smoking logs' effect," added Dad.

This was not good news. As long as Mom and Dad fussed over their make-believe diorama of our last adventure, we wouldn't be going out on any *new* adventures. And we were itching for action. We Kidd kids wanted to jump back into the field and hunt some new treasures.

Mom and Dad?

They thought it was their job to "educate and enlighten the public" on the plight of the rain forest.

Yep. That's what'll happen when both your parents are super-genius professors with multiple PhDs (in addition to their mad spy skills). They want to educate everybody they meet.

Meanwhile, we were stuck. In a city. In an apartment! We're used to sleeping on boats or in tents or under the stars.

"You guys," groused Beck, slamming down her knife and fork dramatically, "we haven't been on a real treasure hunt in months."

"We're bored," I added.

"Have you finished all of your homework?" asked Mom because she's also the professor in charge of our homeschooling.

"We had homework?" said Tommy.

"Washington, DC is full of history," said Mom. "You four should get out and explore it."

"It'll give you kids something exciting and thrilling to do," said Dad. "School groups come to DC all the time. There's so much to see.

The Lincoln Memorial. The White House. The National Gallery of Art."

"They do have a da Vinci *and* a Raphael," said Beck, softening. She, of course, is our resident *artiste* so she's a sucker for art galleries.

"I'd like to visit the Library of Congress," said Storm. "See if they need any help cataloging their collection..."

"I want to go to the International Spy Museum," I said because, hey, I did.

So, we all agreed to stop whining. We'd take a break from treasure hunting. We'd give DC a chance.

The next day, while Mom and Dad reworked the "smoldering logs" section of their Smithsonian exhibit, we checked out all the major tourist attractions. Storm, of course, was our walking, talking guidebook.

"George Washington never lived in Washington, DC. There's a bathtub in the basement of the Capitol building. The White House has thirty-five bathrooms and until 1901, it used to be called the 'Executive Residence'...."

THE ANDREW JACKSON STATUE ACROSS FROM THE WHITE HOUSE WAS PARTIALLY MADE FROM BRITISH CANNONS TAKEN IN THE WAR OF 1812!

THERE'S A DARTH VADER GARGOYLE ADORNING THE NATIONAL CATHEDRAL.

THE BRONZE STATUE OF FREEDOM ATOP THE CAPITOL DOME IS NINE-TEEN FEET TALL AND WEIGHS 15,000 POUNDS.

By the middle of the afternoon, three of us were seriously bored. There's only so much white marble you can stare at. There's only so much trivia we can listen to our big sister blather.

"Here's an interesting tidbit of little-known history," said Storm, the only one of us still enjoying the sightseeing. "Right before World War Two, curators at the Smithsonian and the National

Gallery of Art feared that Washington, DC would become the target of a bombing blitz, just like the one over in London."

"So?" I said grouchily (because my feet were tired).

"So," said Storm, "they came up with a plan to build a super-secret bomb shelter vault underneath the Oliver Wendell Holmes Jr. Memorial to hide the country's most valuable treasures."

Treasures?

Okay. Storm definitely had our attention again.

CHAPTER 6

"Who's this Oliver Wendell Holmes dude?" asked Tommy. "Any relation to Sherlock?"

"Um, no," said Beck (because she and I went to more homeschool history classes than Tommy). "He was like a major Supreme Court Justice. 1902 to 1932."

"Oh, right," said Tommy. "The scowling dude with the walrus mustache."

"Unfortunately," said Storm, "the secret treasure vault was never built."

"Says who?" I asked.

"History," replied Storm.

Tommy nodded. "History. It knows *everything*

that ever happened."

"Or, maybe," I said, "the phrase 'it was never built' is just super-secret spy lingo for 'it *was* built!'"

"Exactly!" said Beck. "That's how you guard treasures. You deny that you're guarding them!"

"Seriously?" said Tommy.

"It's the old deny-it-to-hide-it trick," I said.

"That is so clever," said Tommy. "I wish I'd thought of it."

"You guys?" said Storm. "Are you thinking what I think you're thinking?"

"Yes," I said. "It's time for another treasure hunt. A real one!"

"First stop," said Beck, "the Oliver Wendell Holmes Jr. Memorial!"

"Let's go!" I hollered. "Lead the way, Storm."

Our big sister didn't budge.

"Um, I couldn't find one on any map of DC."

"Wow!" I said. "It's that big of a secret? That means it has to be the classified entrance to a clandestine treasure vault!"

"Not really," said Beck.

I glared at her. She glared at me. Maybe it

was because we were tired of walking around Washington. Maybe we were hangry because we'd passed up several hot dog carts on our wanderings. Maybe it was just time for us to explode.

Because, right there, in front of Abraham Lincoln and a tourist group from Boise, Idaho, we launched into Twin Tirade number 2001. Our TTs, in case you've never witnessed one, are rapid-fire outbursts of anger between Beck and me that evaporate faster than a spilled droplet of canteen water in the Mojave Desert. We sizzle for a few

seconds, let off a little steam, and then, *POOF,* there's nothing left. Usually, we even forget what we were so steamed up about.

"If the Oliver Wendell Holmes Jr. Memorial was real," shouted Beck, "it'd be on a map!"

"Not if the people who built the national treasure vault underneath it wanted to keep it a secret!"

"You mean like how Mom and Dad should've kept you a secret?"

"Kids don't go on maps!"

"Yes, they do," insisted Beck. "They're called family trees!"

"Oh, you're right," I realized. "Those are genealogical maps."

"And you and I are right next to each other."

"Hanging out on the same branch."

"Like two leaves."

"Or two nuts," said Storm, who usually doesn't get involved in our twin tirades. She and Tommy know to hang back and let Beck and me just tantrum it out for a few seconds.

But this was different.

Tourists were staring at us.

So was a young park ranger in a Smokey Bear hat.

She had her eyes on us.

Meanwhile, Tommy had *his* eyes on her.

CHAPTER 7

"Well, hello, there," Tommy said to the cute park ranger. "I bet George Washington would cross the Delaware all over again if you were on the other side."

The ranger grinned and rolled her eyes.

"Is everything okay?" she asked.

"That depends," said Tommy. "Do you believe in love at first sight or should I leave and come back?"

Yep. There's a reason Mom and Dad call our big brother Tailspin Tommy. Whenever he sees a pretty girl he nosedives hopelessly into love faster than a paper airplane made out of soggy cardboard.

The ranger laughed and said, "Are you Tommy Kidd? Member of the famous Kidd Family Explorers?"

"Chya," said Tommy, wiggling his eyebrows proudly, like he wasn't surprised that somebody actually recognized him (which, hello, nobody ever does). "Guilty as charged."

"I'm so looking forward to your exhibit at the Smithsonian."

"Huh?" said Tommy.

"The thing Mom and Dad are doing?" I said, trying to help Tommy out. He's really good at first lines with girls. The second and third? Not so much.

"Oh, right. The exhibit. Peru. The quest for the city of gold. Paititi. We found it. We hunt treasures. That's why they call us treasure hunters."

Yes, Tommy was babbling like an idiot.

"Tommy was almost sacrificed to the ancient Incan gods," said Storm. "Me, too. It was a fun trip. Special."

"Hey," I said, "you're a National Park Ranger!"

"Really?" said the girl, whose nametag ID'ed

her as Rachel G. "What gave me away? The floppy hat or the stylish khaki clothes?"

"We need help!" said Beck.

"You mean like a counselor or school psychiatrist?"

"Huh?"

"I saw you two screaming at each other."

"Oh, that was just a twin tirade," I said. "We do those all the time. They're no biggy. No, what we need is some information. Where exactly is the Oliver Wendell Holmes J. Memorial?"

"It's not on the map," said Storm.

"Because it doesn't exist," said Park Ranger Rachel.

Beck licked her finger and marked an invisible 1 in the air. Okay. She was right. Score one for team Beck.

"They were supposed to build it but never did," Rachel explained.

"Oh," I said, defeated. "Guess they didn't build the other thing, either."

"What other thing?"

"It's a secret."

"No," said Beck, "it's a joke."

"Whatever."

"Hey," said Rachel, "you guys like quirky adventures, am I right?"

"Totally," said Tommy. "What kind of movies do you like? The ones with singing troll dolls? Because we're not really busy and I was thinking maybe you and I—"

"Sorry," said Rachel. "I'm super-busy. But since you guys like secrets and hidden treasures, you might have fun looking for this."

She handed us a business card. There was a shiny silver eagle embossed in the corner and a photo of a pyramid in a hole.

"Huh," I said, when it was my turn to check out the photo. "It looks like the top of a miniature Washington Monument."

"Yep," said Rachel. "Because that's exactly what it is!"

"Where is it?"

"Ah, you'll need to figure that out."

CHAPTER 8

There was a riddle printed on the back of the small card.

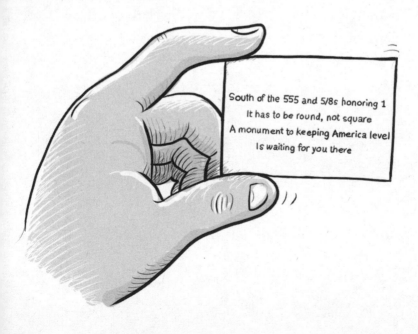

South of the 555 and 5/8s honoring 1
It has to be round, not square
A monument to keeping America level
Is waiting for you there

"It's an old riddle," said the park ranger. "Been around since the early 1940s, I'm told. Not many people know about it. But, well, I figure I can trust you guys. You Kidds are national treasures."

"Really?" said Tommy, blushing. "We are?"

"Totally. I've been super-impressed by all your adventures." The National Park Ranger gave us a crisp salute off the brim of her hat. "Happy hunting."

"Wow," said Tommy, meekly. "I think she likes me." He tucked the card into a zippered pocket on his safari vest. "I'm going to keep her card close to my heart forever."

"Can we crack the riddle first?" I said.

"The first line is easy," said Storm, who didn't need to reread the card because she'd already memorized the clue. "The Washington Monument is a five-hundred-and-fifty-five-foot-and-five-eighth-inches tall obelisk honoring number one—George Washington, the first president of the United States."

"Seriously?" said Beck. "You knew that?"

Storm shrugged and tapped her temple. "I mentally photocopied the guidebook in our hotel room."

"So, we need to be south of the Washington Monument," I said.

We raced down the steps of the Lincoln Memorial, along the sides of the reflecting pool, past the World War II memorial, and onto the looping sidewalks south of the Washington Monument.

"Now what are we looking for?" I asked.

"Something that has to be round," replied Storm. "Not square."

"A pizza!" blurted Tommy.

"Sicilian pizzas are rectangles," said Beck.

"Rectangles aren't squares," said Tommy.

"But all squares are rectangles," I reminded him.

"Maybe. But a pizza would taste good right now. Regular *or* Sicilian."

"It's a manhole cover!" said Beck.

"Exactly," said Storm. "Manhole covers need to be round. If they were square, you could, potentially, drop the lid down the hole."

"There!" I said, pointing to a manhole cover in the grassy lawn.

We hopped over the low chain fence and ran to it.

It took several grunts, but the four of us pried open the manhole cover.

There it was. Right under the lid. A replica of the Washington Monument, hidden in an underground brick chimney.

"What about that line in the riddle about keeping things level?" I asked.

"Of course!" said Storm, who must've flipped through the stack of mental note cards in her head. "This five-foot-tall model of the monument is officially known as Benchmark A, a geodetic control point used by surveyors."

"Huh?" Beck, Tommy, and I said together.

"Geodetic control points provide starting points for maps. This mini monument was probably placed here in the 1880s as part of a transcontinental leveling program!"

"Hey, check it out," said Tommy. "It looks like you can twist the top..."

He reached down into the hole but froze the instant somebody shouted, "Vandals! Leave that alone!"

It was another park ranger. An older guy. Maybe in his eighties. Maybe older.

He came charging across the grass. Actually, he was chugging. He was also wheezing.

It didn't seem like the old guy thought we Kidds were national treasures. More like national nuisances.

CHAPTER 9

"**D**ude," said Tommy, as he let the old guy lean against his chest to catch his breath. "Are you seriously a park ranger?"

"Semi-retired!" snapped the old man. "But I'm still on the lookout for troublemaking whipper-snappers like you four young hooligans!"

"Another park ranger told us about this hidden treasure," I tried to explain.

"Where are your parents?" snapped the ranger.

"At the, uh, Smithsonian," said Tommy.

"What?" said the old man. "Who are they? The Lindberghs?"

"No," I said, "we're the Kidd Family Treasure Hunters. We're doing an exhibit about our time in Peru."

"Is that so? What'd you kids break down there in South America?"

"A dam," said Tommy. "And a lake, I guess."

"But," I said, sort of defensively, "we found Paititi, the lost city of gold."

"Well there's no gold down there," he said, gesturing toward the open manhole. "Best you forget you ever found this little DC secret."

"But the other ranger gave us a card," said Storm. "Surely, if you folks didn't want people to find this mini monument, you wouldn't have a riddle about how to find it printed up on business cards."

"What was her name?" asked the ranger.

Tommy was about to blurt it out (because he's super-innocent that way). I cut him off.

"None of your beeswax!" I shouted.

"Strange name," said the old man, narrowing his eyes at me.

"We're treasure hunters," I told him. "We don't reveal our sources."

"Except in matters of vital national security," said Storm. "Which, we must assume, this is not."

The old man's eye began to twitch. "There's nothing to see here. Nothing at all. Move along. Move along."

"But I wanted to twist the pyramid top," said Tommy.

"I said, move along!"

"What seems to be the trouble, Gus?" asked a uniformed DC cop who strolled over to us.

"Nothing, Latoya. Just some rug rats poking their noses into places where they ought not to be poking them."

The cop turned to us. "Gus here is ninety-two," she said. "Oldest park ranger in DC. If he tells you to move along, you move along."

Storm's eyes grew dark and cloudy. Seriously. That's why Mom nicknamed her Storm. When she gets mad, it's like an angry typhoon billows up inside her and blows away everything in its path.

"Excuse me, officer," said Storm, taking a bold step forward. "Since I don't see any *no trespassing* signs, aren't we within our constitutional rights to walk across the grass and open a manhole cover so we can gaze down into a sewer?"

"It's actually more like a buried chimney," I said. "Or a well..."

The police officer hiked up her gun belt. "Where are your parents, little lady?"

Oh, no.

The police officer called Storm "little lady."

Storm finds that very demeaning, patronizing, and condescending.

So, if you do it, prepare for the fury of what we call the Category Five Storm (where there will be severe anger, drenching rage, and serious damage to anything in her path).

And that's how we ended up riding over to see Mom and Dad at the Smithsonian in the backseat of a police cruiser.

CHAPTER 10

"**T**hank you, officer," said Dad.

"It won't happen again," said Mom.

Dad shook the officer's hand. "We'll keep a better eye on them. We promise."

"See that you do," said the officer.

Storm was still mad. If she were a cartoon, whistling steam would be teakettling out of her ears. "But the other ranger...Rachel..."

Dad held up a hand. "That's enough, Stephanie."

Yes, that's her real name. But only Mom and Dad can call her that.

"We'll be keeping the children on a shorter leash," said Mom.

"Wha?" said Tommy, rubbing his neck. "We have to wear leashes?"

"It's only a figure of speech, son," said Dad.

"Ohhhh. One of those. Got it."

The police officer finally left. When she was gone, Dad announced, "Family meeting."

"Here?" I asked, because there were workers crawling all over the Paititi exhibit, gluing tiny Incans to the miniature mountains. Usually, we like to keep our Kidd family business private. Especially when we're about to be disciplined, which I figured we were.

"No," said Mom. "Back at the apartment. Let's take a break, Thomas."

Dad nodded. "Right you are, Sue."

They packed up their briefcases and we hiked the seven blocks in silence.

We filed into the apartment and found our usual seats in the living room. By the way, we've never really had a living room before. It'd be a waste of space on a boat. When we were on adventures, we were too busy actually living to need a room dedicated to it.

"Children," said Dad, "here's the situation. Your mother and I must remain here in Washington for at least six more weeks."

"We have to repair and complete the exhibit," added Mom. "Plus, we promised the Smithsonian and our friends in Peru that we would host a series of lectures about the plight of the Amazon rain forest."

"Therefore," said Dad, "we cannot take you kids on another grand exploration."

"Although we certainly wish we could," said Mom.

Dad nodded. "I, like you, chafe at city living."

Tommy raised his hand.

"Yes, Tommy?"

"Does that mean you don't like it?"

"Indeed. I'd much rather be on board *The Lost,* sailing to parts unknown. Or in the jungle. Or scaling a mountain."

"But," said Mom, "commitments are commitments."

"So," said Storm, "we're stuck here, too?"

"We're just supposed to sit around and do nothing?" I said.

Mom looked at Dad, who had just turned to look at her.

"Not necessarily," said Dad.

"I have an uncle," said Mom.

"A spy?" said Beck. "Like weird Uncle Timothy?"

Mom shook her head. "No. This is a real uncle.

My father's brother. We've never officially intro-duced him to you kids because, well, he's…quite the world traveler."

The way Mom said it, I figured this uncle was "quite" some other stuff, too.

"He's also a gambler," said Dad.

"Yes," said Mom. "There's that. He's also, well, let's just say he's a bit eccentric."

"What's his name?" I asked.

"Richie," said Mom. "Uncle Richie 'Poppie' Luccio."

"'Poppie'?" I said.

"It's his nickname."

"So, you could've called him Uncle Poppie?" said Tommy.

"No," said Storm. "That would just be confusing."

"True," said Mom. "Uncle Richie took me on my first dig back when I was younger than Bick and Beck. It just so happens that he's in Washing-ton right now."

"Cool!" I said. "Is he here on another big dig?"

"No," said Mom. "It, uh, has something to do with another big card game."

"Which he lost," added Dad.

"So," said Storm. "He needs the babysitting money?"

Storm. She always blurts out whatever's on her mind whenever it happens to be there.

"Yes," said Mom. "He does. And you four need adult supervision."

Great, I thought. A wacky great-uncle who just lost a ton of money playing poker. I couldn't wait to meet the guy.

And guess what?

We didn't have to.

CHAPTER 11

Two hours later, Uncle Richie strode into the room, toting a sack of groceries.

"Came as swiftly as I could, Susan," he said to Mom. "Even though it meant I had to leave the table earlier than I might have chosen, if you catch my meaning."

"You lost?" said Dad.

"Again?" said Mom.

"Tut, tut. Buck up, you two. It is far, far better to dare mighty things and fail than to rank among those poor souls who neither enjoy nor suffer much because they live in a gray twilight that knows neither victory nor defeat!"

Uncle Richie was a swaggering, blustery man who sort of reminded me of Teddy Roosevelt. You could tell he was a treasure hunter at heart because he was dressed for his next expedition, even if it was just running out to the grocery store.

Uncle Richie puffed up his chest and addressed Mom and Dad as if he were giving a speech. "Thomas? Susan? Although I have no children of my own, rest assured I am fully prepared to shepherd and safeguard your young charges during your extended stay here in the District of Columbia." He turned to us. "Children, as my personal hero, Theodore 'Teddy' Roosevelt..."

(Nailed it.)

"...once said: 'Keep your eyes on the stars and your feet on the ground!'"

"He also said: 'It is hard to fail, but it is worse to never to have tried to succeed,'" said Storm.

"Bully for you! You're Storm, I take it?"

"Yes, sir."

"Excellent. A kindred spirit if ever I saw one. Oh, we shall accomplish great things together, you and I. Daring, courageous, magnificent things!"

"Like skinny-dipping in the Potomac River?" said Storm.

"Ah! I see you know of the particulars of President Roosevelt's time in the White House."

"Yes. He's my hero, too. Well, one of them."

"Bully for you! Bully!"

"Uh, Uncle Richie?" said Mom.

"Yes, Susan?"

"We don't want the kids skinny-dipping in the Potomac."

"Of course not. The Chesapeake Bay would be much more invigorating!"

"Awesome!" said Tommy.

"Uncle Richie?" said Dad, shaking his head.

"Right. No skinny-dipping. Understood." He crisply saluted Dad. "Consider that suggestion erased from my memory. Forget I ever said skinny-dipping. Drat. I said it again!"

I raised my hand.

"Yes, Bickford?"

"You can call me Bick."

"Very well. I shall endeavor to do so."

"How come we've never met you before?"

He gave Mom and Dad a quick glance. "Been busy, lad. Very, very busy. In fact, I was all set to embark on another grand expedition when I received the call from your father and mother."

"We thought you were playing cards," said Beck.

Uncle Richie tapped the side of his head. "For mental stimulation, only, my dear. Mental stimulation."

"Well," said Dad, "we were hoping to head back to the Smithsonian this afternoon...work on our exhibit..."

"As well you should, Thomas. For the best prize that life has to offer is the chance to work hard at work worth doing! Off with you, then. You too, Susan. Your children are in good hands. There's no need to fear, Uncle Richie is here!"

From the look on Mom's face?

I don't think she was totally buying it.

CHAPTER 12

Dad and Mom went back to work. (After giving Uncle Richie all sorts of emergency phone numbers and showing him where the first aid kit and fire extinguisher were located.)

The rest of us went for a brisk hike through the streets of Washington, DC, led by Uncle Richie, who moved at a very vigorous pace. We were all huffing and puffing, just trying to keep up.

"Never, throughout history, has a man who lived a life of ease left a name worth remembering," proclaimed Uncle Richie, pointing one finger to the sky.

"Except for La-Z-Boy," quipped Beck.

"Who?"

"The guy who invented the recliner."

"Happy to say I never met the man," replied Uncle Richie.

"Actually," said Storm. "La-Z-Boy isn't a person. It's a furniture manufacturing company based in Monroe, Michigan."

"Ah! James Monroe. Now there was a president! He really knew how to write a doctrine."

"He also helped negotiate the Louisiana Purchase," added Storm.

"Somebody bought Louisiana?" said Tommy, sounding shocked. "Did they get New Orleans and Mardi Gras, too? Bummer..."

We just ignored him. We sometimes have to.

"Well, now," said Uncle Richie, "it is after noon. The lunch hour draws nigh. However, having never had children of my own, I relied upon my treasure-hunt-honed research skills to locate a suitable, child-friendly restaurant for our dining pleasure. In my quest, I stumbled upon a list of

Washington, DC's most kid-friendly eating establishments on the internet."

"That's cool," said Tommy. "We have our own category on the web. Kidd-friendly."

Beck rolled her eyes. "They probably didn't spell it with two Ds, Tommy."

"Well they should've. Because that's how we spell our name."

"What establishment topped your list, Uncle Richie?" asked Storm.

"A quaint place called Firefly seemed promising. It's over near Dupont Circle. Thirteen-ten New Hampshire Avenue, if memory serves."

Uncle Richie stuck two fingers in his lips and whistled. It was shrill enough to shatter glass. Six taxis screeched to a halt. He opened the door on the first one.

"Well done, good fellow," he said to the driver. "Victory goes to the swift! Pile in, children. Be quick about it. We're off to Firefly!"

The restaurant was nice. There was even a tree in the middle of the dining room.

It was also extremely kid-friendly. The menu included peanut butter, jelly, and banana sandwiches, mac and cheese (with fries or veggie sticks), plus meatballs with buttered noodles.

Every kids' meal also included a cookie to decorate, which you could eat after the server whisked it away to have it baked in the kitchen.

We all just sat there. Looking glum. We let Beck, our family artist, decorate our four cookies. She gave them frowny faces.

"I take it you children are not delighted with my choice of luncheon location?" said Uncle Richie.

"This place is great," I said. "I'm sure the cookies will be delicious."

"But," said Beck, "we're Kidds, not kids."

"There's a difference," said Tommy. "And it's bigger than an extra D."

"I see," said Uncle Richie. "Well then, if you children truly crave excitement more than macaroni and cheese, might I offer a suggestion?"

"Go for it, dude!" said Tommy.

"Let us settle up with our server, leave a generous tip, and hurry over to the Mansion on O Street! I suspect you'll find it much more, as you say, *Kidd*-friendly!"

CHAPTER 13

Turns out the Mansion on O Street was more than a mansion.

The Mansion was more like a museum! A series of five interconnected town houses, it had more than one hundred rooms, including a two-story log cabin. The ceilings were hand painted in all sorts of styles. There were stained glass windows everywhere, an Art Deco penthouse with a private elevator, plus all sorts of memorabilia, including guitars autographed by rock stars like the Rolling Stones.

"This mansion is steeped with history," said Uncle Richie. "Nearly every president since my favorite, Teddy Roosevelt, has visited. J. Edgar Hoover's G-men lived here at one point. And the mother of the civil rights movement, Rosa Parks, called the Mansion her home whenever she visited DC. The Mansion is an excellent place to sharpen one's treasure-hunting skills. There are seventy secret doors and many hidden passages. The Mansion is a veritable maze! However, there is no map! You must find your way through the zany labyrinth using nothing but cunning, wit, and guile!"

Uncle Richie quickly arranged for us to take a self-guided tour even though we were last minute drop-ins.

"The manager is an old friend of mine," he told us. "Let's just say he owes me a favor and leave it at that, shall we?"

We started roaming around, going through secret doors that led to other rooms, staircases, and closets.

One door was a bookcase filled with knick-knacks that led us into the house next door. Another was a pantry that slid sideways. A bunch were mirrors. We found about eight doors each. Way above average. But, then again—we *are* professional treasure hunters.

When we were exhausted from exploring all the nooks and crannies and Beatles memorabilia

and chandeliers and the Rosa Parks room and
EVERYTHING, we headed down to the restaurant where they let us eat waffles and bacon for a
late afternoon snack.

Seems Uncle Richie knew the restaurant manager, too.

"Was that a bit more to your liking?" asked
Uncle Richie with a sly grin as he speared a
wedge of waffle.

70

"Totally," said Tommy, wolfing down six pieces of bacon because he, like all of us, was starving after running around the Mansion (not to mention up and down all its staircases) for a couple hours.

"But," said Beck, "as fun as it was..."

Uncle Richie nodded. "I know, Rebecca. I know. There's nothing like the thrill of an actual adventure! To be out in the field, chasing down clues, finding a true treasure that most consider lost to the ages. Why, I remember when I discovered the mummy of Kittentomen..."

"Whoa," said Tommy. "You discovered a mummy?"

"Indeed. And his whole tomb. Filled with riches. Gold vessels. Jewels. Precious objects. All of which, of course, I donated to the nearest museum."

"Was that the dig you took Mom on when she was a kid?" I asked.

"Yes."

"Is she the one who made you donate all the treasure to the locals?"

Uncle Richie nodded. "Yes. And she was only seven years old. Your mother looked up at me with those big, blue eyes and, well, how could I refuse her anything? Besides, it was the honorable and virtuous thing to do!"

"Uncle Richie?" I said.

"Yes, Bickford?"

"You're supposed to call me Bick. Remember?"

"Ah, yes. My bad."

"And I'm Beck."

"Right you are, Rebecca. What was your question, Bick?"

"Were you really about to set off on another expedition? A treasure hunt?"

Uncle Richie rubbed his hands together. "Indeed so. For certain information has recently fallen into my possession. Information that could very well lead me to..."

He paused dramatically. In my head, I could hear the *dun-dun-dun*s.

"The Lost Ship of the Desert!"

CHAPTER 14

"There's a treasure ship?" I said. "Lost in the desert?"

"Well, duh," said Tommy. "If it's a boat and it's in the desert then it's totally lost, little bro."

"There are several legends about maritime vessels stranded in the deserts of the American Southwest," said Storm.

"But how'd they get there?" asked Beck.

"Bad boat drivers," said Tommy, who is excellent at skippering our ship, *The Lost.*

Uncle Richie got a twinkle in his eyes and leaned across the table to recite a memorized verse.

A mountaineer, storm-stained and brown,
From farthest desert touched the town.
And, striding along, held up,
Above his head, a jeweled cup!

"Whoa," said Tommy. "Pirate poetry! My fave."

Uncle Richie kept going.

"He whispered wild, and said with lifted hand,
'Doubloons are sown along the sand!'"

"Seriously?" said Beck. "Some wheezy old sun-baked geezer stumbled into a town and started rhyming at people about doubloons lying in the sand?"

Uncle Richie gave her a mischievous grin. "So it is written in Joaquin Miller's 1875 book *The Ship in the Desert*! But what I am searching for is the lost pearl ship of Spanish Explorer Juan de Iturbe. It was a shallow-drafted caravel—"

"Making it the size of Christopher Columbus's smaller ships," added Storm.

"Exactly!" said Uncle Richie. "You see, Señor Juan de Iturbe was on a pearl-harvesting expedition up the Gulf of California."

"That's between the Baja Peninsula and mainland Mexico," said Storm. (She and Uncle Richie made quite a team.)

"Precisely!" said Uncle Richie. "A king tide—which, of course, is very high—coupled with a storm surge carried his ship across a strait and propelled that vessel more than one hundred miles northward, far up into what is now California, near present-day San Diego. The pearl-hunting ship was soon deposited in a distant saltwater basin—a lake in the process of drying up. Eventually, that dead lake would create part of what we now know as the Salton Sea basin at the northern edge of the Sonora Desert."

Tommy nodded. "That'll happen in the desert. Lakes will dry up on you."

"After exploring the lake for several days," Uncle Richie continued, "Señor de Iturbe came to the unfortunate but undeniable conclusion that he would not be able to sail out again. His ship's keel was stuck in a sandbar. So, with no good options, he abandoned his craft. Standing upright, it looked as if it were still sailing across the windswept ocean of sand. He and his entire crew hiked back across the desert to the nearest Spanish settlement, leaving behind a fortune in precious black pearls!"

*SOMEBODY TRY TO REMEMBER WHERE WE PARKED OUR BOAT!

"And nobody's ever discovered the ship?" I asked.

"Nobody," said Uncle Richie.

"So, you want to go to the desert to find Señor de Iturbe's ship?"

"Indeed, Bick, I do. For, I suspect its hull will be heavy with treasure chests, all of them laden with priceless black pearls!"

"But," said Beck, "all you have to work with is a legend!"

"True. However, sometimes, a legend is all we need!"

CHAPTER 15

U ncle Richie suggested we stroll over to Dupont Circle to catch a cab back to our apartment.

"I'd like to stop by Second Story Books," he said. "It's only a two-minute walk from here. They have a marvelous collection of rare and out-of-print books. I might be able to locate a gently used copy of Joaquin Miller's epic poem. Research for the expedition, eh?"

So, once again, we tried to keep up with Uncle Richie, who was unusually athletic and spry for a guy in his seventies. Second Story Books had a series of rolling bookcases set up on the sidewalk in front of their shop. Browsers were searching the shelves—readers lost in their own treasure hunts.

"I'll only be a moment," said Uncle Richie.

"Can I search with you?" asked Storm.

"Why, I'd be delighted for the company!"

They headed into the bookshop.

"I want to see if they have any rare sailing books," said Tommy.

He went in to browse, too.

Leaving Beck and me on the sidewalk with the bargain hunters pawing through the books lined up on the rolling carts.

I recognized one of the shoppers because the sun was reflecting off his bald dome. Yep. It was that Professor Hingleburt, the stuffy guy who gave Mom and Dad grief when we were running around like wild things on our quest to find the Hope Diamond.

"Did you hear?" Dr. Hingleburt said to the man and woman browsing with him. "The Kidds are in town."

ANNOYING GROWN UP ALERT! NOBODY DO ANYTHING FUN.

"Who are the Kidds?" asked the man.

"You know. Drs. Thomas and Susan Kidd. The treasure hunters who gallivant about the globe with their children, looking for long-lost treasures while simultaneously fighting to protect the environment."

"Oh, yes," said the lady, looking down her nose. "I've heard about them. Aren't they doing something at the Smithsonian?"

"Yes," said Dr. Hingleburt. "An exhibit about their discoveries in Peru. The Lost City of Paititi."

"That's a hoax," said the lady.

"They claim they found it," said Dr. Hingleburt, with a dismissive shrug. "I suppose the Smithsonian will let anybody say whatever they want—as long as it sells tickets."

I looked at Beck. She looked at me. Both of us were clenching our fists and grinding our teeth. It's another twin thing. Somebody talks trash about our family, we get mad.

"Of course, you know whom Mrs. Kidd is related to," sniffed Hingleburt.

"Whom?" said the lady.

"The infamous Richie 'Poppie' Luccio! He's her uncle."

"That old fool?" said the lady.

"The same."

"Remember, a dozen years ago, when that museum in Sydney gave him back all the treasure he originally claimed came from a 1622 shipwreck off the coast of Australia?" said the man. "Richie Luccio recanted the entire tale! Admitted it was totally made up."

"How could I forget?" said Dr. Hingleburt, chortling merrily.

Beck and I were about to march over there and give these snooty Washingtonians a piece of our mind.

But that's when Tommy, Storm, and Uncle Richie came out of the bookstore with their purchases.

"Well, speak of the devil!" said Professor Hingleburt, who'd just seen and recognized Uncle Richie. "Off on another grand treasure hunt, Poppie?"

"Perhaps, Henry," said Uncle Richie. "Perhaps."

"Will you give it all back again?" asked the lady. Then she and her pals started tittering and giggling.

"Come on, Uncle Richie," I said, running over and grabbing his hand while Beck grabbed the other one. "Let's go home and eat some of that ice cream you bought."

"Yeah," said Beck.

We pulled him away from the snickering snobs as quickly as we could.

But I glanced up and caught a glimpse of his face. That was the first time I'd seen Uncle Richie look sad.

I also hoped it would be the last.

CHAPTER 16

Mom and Dad were home when we returned to the apartment.

"We're going to eat ice cream!" I announced. "Chunky Monkey! Rocky Road!" I said the flavors as boisterously as Uncle Richie had announced them when he first walked through our door.

But he still wasn't smiling.

"Ah, Thomas. Susan. Good to see you." Uncle Richie sounded like the weary old man he could've been. "Your children are a joy and a delight. It was grand spending time with them."

"Thank you so much, Uncle Richie," said Mom.

"Are you free tomorrow?" asked Dad.

"Unfortunately, no. You see, Thomas, I am setting off on a new expedition." He thumped the hard cover of the antique book he'd just bought. "I'll be searching for the Lost Ship of the Desert! I have a few promising leads. Very promising, indeed."

"They're solid?" asked Dad, sounding impressed.

"As solid as any I've ever followed."

Mom nodded politely when he said that. "Good, Uncle Richie. Good."

"Flying off to California tomorrow. I'll be touching down at a secluded airstrip I know of near the Salton Sea, not far from San Diego, as the crow flies. I've made preliminary arrangements with a local excavating company to borrow a backhoe and bulldozer. Might need to dig my way through several hundred years of sand."

"Do you have the money to finance your expedition?" asked Dad.

"I am in the process of securing funding," said Uncle Richie.

That sounded like he was off to another card game.

"Can we go find the buried treasure with you?"

asked Tommy. "I mean, Mom and Dad are going to be busy. We're going to be bored."

"It would be an honor to excavate sand alongside you, sir," said Storm. "I mean, Uncle Richie."

"Love to have you along, Thomas. You, too, Storm."

"I want to go, too," I said.

"Bully for you, Bick. Bully."

"We could finance the trip," said Mom.

"We'd be happy to do it," added Dad. "I've been curious about the legendary Lost Ship of the Desert for quite some time."

Beck was the only one in the room not saying anything.

"Well," said Uncle Richie, who had to notice Beck's silence (it was hard not to). "Talk it over amongst yourselves. I'd love to have you children along for the ride. It would prove to be a marvelous expedition, I'm sure. I hope to be wheels-up at nine hundred hours. Please let me know ASAP if you will be joining me on this quest. Life is a grand adventure, children. Accept it in such a spirit, and it doesn't matter what the naysayers buying bargain books along the boulevard might blather about you!"

Uncle Richie had bucked himself back up. He tipped his hat and strode triumphantly out the door.

The instant he was gone, I turned to Beck.

"Can we have the room?" I said to everybody else.

"Of course," said Mom. She, Dad, Storm, and Tommy went off to the kitchen to start scooping ice cream. They knew what was brewing.

EAT YOUR ICE CREAM **FAST**, EVERYBODY. WE MIGHT JUST MELT iT WiTH OUR **RED-HOT FURY.**

"Do you have a problem, Rebecca?" I shouted.

"Of course, I do. You're my brother."

"I meant about Uncle Richie!"

"He's full of hot air!"

"So are balloons, and they can take you places you've never been before."

"They can also burst in midair and leave you stranded in the desert!"

"Oh, so you're afraid?" I said.

"You heard Professor Hingleburt! He said Uncle Richie is a phony and a fraud."

"Ha!" I scoffed. "Talk about hot air. Hingleburt has so much, he scorched off his own hair. That's why he's bald."

"I know," said Beck. "How dare he talk about our family like that! We're the Kidds. So is Uncle Richie."

"Actually, he's a Luccio, like Mom used to be. But he's still family!"

"Right. Good catch, Bick."

"Thanks, Beck. All for one and one for all!"

"You're right. So, what are we doing yelling at each other?"

"I have absolutely no idea. Especially since we need to start packing!"

Beck nodded. "Nine hundred hours is early."

"I know! It's like nine o'clock in the morning."

"Because it *is* nine o'clock in the morning."

"Good point."

"Thank you."

I turned to the kitchen.

"You guys?" I hollered. "We need to load up our gear. Hurry up and finish your dessert. We're going to the desert with Uncle Richie!"

CHAPTER 17

The next morning, we were airborne at promptly 9 a.m.

"Punctuality is the politeness of kings," said Uncle Richie over the roar of the engines after we lifted off from the private aviation center at DC's Dulles airport.

"King Louis the eighteenth of France said that," said Storm.

"Indeed, he did. Bully for you, Storm. Bully!"

"Whoa, there were, like, seventeen Louies before him?" said Tommy. "What's wrong with

France? Don't they have any other good first names for kings?"

Once again, we ignored him.

Maybe because Storm, Beck, and I were scared. The twin-propeller plane was lurching forward, with one wing and then the other taking the lead.

"Uncle Richie?" I said over the rattle and hum of the groaning engines. "How old is this aircraft?"

"It's not old, Bick. It's gently used. Ladies and gentlemen, you are now flying in a 1971 Piper Aztec. It's the very same twin-engine plane that the record-shattering British aviatrix Sheila Scott once flew around the world the longitudinal way—by flying over both poles!"

"Wow!" said Tommy, who'd been studying for his pilot license. "This used to be her plane?" He did have another reason for that nickname of his.

"Perhaps," said Uncle Richie. "I did find an interesting pair of ladies' boots in the cargo bay when I took possession of it in New Jersey several months ago."

"Did you win it in a card game?" asked Storm, bracing her hands on the back of Tommy's copilot seat as we bumped along.

"Indeed. That's why I call her *The Royal Flush!*"

"But will it make it all the way to California?" asked Beck.

"I certainly hope so," said Uncle Richie as the left engine shook and banged like it wanted to spit out its rivets. "But the suspense of not knowing makes the ride much more interesting, eh?"

Not really, I wanted to say. Instead, I just closed my eyes.

We chugged along without incident for two hours.

"Anyone care for a loop-de-loop?" asked Uncle Richie when we were somewhere over Tennessee. I think he was bored.

"Go for it!" shouted Tommy before the rest of us could scream, *"No!"*

"Cheerio!" cried Uncle Richie. "Hang on to your hats, your backpacks, and your breakfasts!"

When we finally pulled out of the loop, Beck and I turned to Storm.

"Are we there yet?" we gasped.

Storm shook her head. "One thousand nine hundred and nine more miles to go."

"How about a barrel roll, boys and girls?" asked Uncle Richie.

"No!" the three of us shouted before Tommy could shout, "Yes!"

"Very well," said Uncle Richie, "we'll do a hammerhead stall turn coupled with a tail slide instead. You'll see, children. These prop planes are quite nimble. Much more aerobatic than their jet-engine-equipped cousins!"

Yes. It was as scary as you could imagine. Like being on a roller coaster without a track or guardrails.

Tommy loved it. The rest of us remembered our prayers. We knew we were in the hands of a madman. We were never going to find the Lost Ship of the Desert. Instead, we were going to become the Lost Airplane of Wherever We Crashed.

"How about lunch?" Beck shouted after Uncle Richie concluded his stomach-churning display of aerial tumbling and twisting. Lunch, of course, was the last thing on our minds since our stomachs had been tossed around and ended up somewhere behind our noses. But Beck hoped food would distract Uncle Richie from his daredevil actions for at least thirty minutes.

"Bully!" said Uncle Richie. "Unwrap those sandwiches your father packed. Flying upside down can really work up an appetite."

"There's potato salad, too," I said. "And chips. And pickles."

"And fruit," added Beck. "Lots and lots of fruit."

We both wanted this to be a very long lunch. One that might carry us the rest of the way to California without any more flying circus stunts.

Our plan worked.

We cruised across the country without incident. Uncle Richie found a new distraction: teaching Tommy how to fly his 1971 clunker of an airplane. We were all grateful for that.

Until we crossed over the desert and began our initial descent into the Salton Sea area.

That's when Uncle Richie turned to Tommy and said the most terrifying words of them all.

"The controls are yours, Thomas. Bring us in for a landing!"

CHAPTER 18

"So, I just like push this thing forward, right?"

And, just like that, Tailspin Tommy put us into a nosedive.

"Ease back on the yoke, Tommy," said Uncle Richie.

"No problemo. Uh, where exactly is 'the yoke'?"

"In your hands."

"This thing that looks like a steering wheel?"

"Exactly! Well done, lad!"

While Tommy took what I hoped wasn't a "crash course" in landing an airplane, those of us seated in the back were white-knuckling our armrests and tightening our seat belts.

"Don't forget to lower your landing gear," coached Uncle Richie.

"Chya. Definitely," said Tommy. "Can't land without landing gear. Uh, any tips on how to do that?"

"Press the button for wheels-down."

"Oh. Right. Duh."

"Increase flaps ten degrees," said Uncle Richie. "We're coming in too fast."

You know that screaming, whining noises the spaceships in Star Wars movies always make when they're about to crash into the surface of a distant planet? Uncle Richie's plane was making those.

"Um, maybe you should take the wheel," said Tommy.

"Believe you can do it and you're halfway there!" said Uncle Richie. "You've got this, Tommy!"

I looked to Storm. She was shaking her head and mouthing the words, "No, he doesn't."

"Easy, easy," said Uncle Richie. "Keep a nice steady rate of descent. Line up your approach vector. Easy..."

I just closed my eyes.

A few seconds later, I sprang up in my seat. Tommy had found the runway and bounced off it like a rubber ball. But then he chopped the power and we landed again. In fact, we kept bounding up and down the runway like a hopping kangaroo. It was enough to make you want to toss your cookies. Fortunately, there hadn't been any cookies in our lunch sack. Just all that fruit. So, we barfed our bananas when Tommy finally slammed on the brakes and pitched the prop plane into a skittering, skidding, sideways stop.

"Well done, Thomas!" said Uncle Richie. "Bully." Then he turned around to compliment Beck and me on our projectile vomit. "Well aimed, you two. Well aimed, indeed!"

We'd both emptied our stomachs into a quickly improvised air sickness bag: the big brown grocery bag Dad had packed our lunch in.

"Storm?" said Uncle Richie. "Kindly tell everybody where we are."

"The Salton Sea Airport," she replied, as her face slowly lost its pea-green color. "We're a mile southwest of Salton City in Imperial County, California and approximately one hundred and twenty miles northeast of San Diego. The runway is made out of gravel."

"Probably why it was such a bumpy landing," said Tommy.

Riiiight, I thought. *That's why it was so bumpy.*

"Kindly taxi over to that Quonset hut," said Uncle Richie, pointing to a rusty, semicircular, steel building sitting in the middle of a patch of dirt. "Your parents' generous financial support of our expedition allowed me to, late last night,

99

make a few phone calls to an old friend and rent all the gear we might possibly need for our treasure quest in the deserts west and south of here."

I was still feeling pretty queasy. And my legs were kind of wobbly when we finally climbed out of the parked plane and marched across the parched dirt to the storage building.

But once we stepped inside the building and saw what was inside, I forgot all about the rough landing and started to smile. Because we had two awesome ATVs and the coolest RV I've ever seen!

But that wasn't all. Hitched behind the RV was a trailer hauling a backhoe.

"Now, then," said Uncle Richie, "who wants to go play with these toys in a giant sandbox?"

We all shot up our hands.

Hey, even if we didn't find the treasure, we'd sure have a ton of fun trying to dig it up!

CHAPTER 19

Tommy called "first dibs" on the backhoe.

Beck and I hopped into the ATVs while Storm checked out the air-conditioning in the RV.

"It's perfect!" she reported.

Which was a good thing, because we were heading west into the Anza-Borrego Desert, where summertime temperatures average over 100 degrees during the day.

"There's a state park there," said Uncle Richie. "And several camping sites. We'll make that our base as we gather intelligence and pinpoint the precise location of Señor Juan de Iturbe's lost pearl ship!"

Tommy and Storm rode with Uncle Richie in the RV. Beck and I took the ATVs, which were basically overgrown go-karts. We could drive them without a license, as long as we stayed off the roads, which we had absolutely no trouble doing!

We set up camp at the state park in a canyon full of sage brush and scrubby little trees.

And, of course, Storm immediately launched into a tour guide info dump. She is our walking, talking Wikipedia.

"Anza-Borrego gets its name from two sources," she told us. "The eighteenth-century Spanish explorer Juan Bautista de Anza and *borrego,* the Spanish word for bighorn sheep."

"Was Señor Anza a shepherd?" asked Tommy.

"No," said Uncle Richie. "He was an explorer. However, this desert is home to many endangered bighorned sheep."

Storm babbled on about how the park was the second biggest in the contiguous United States. That means all of them except Alaska and Hawaii. Yep, she explained contiguous, too.

A park ranger cruised into our campsite in a Jeep.

"Hi, folks," he said. "What's with the backhoe? Don't see many campers hauling those."

"We're going exploring!" replied Uncle Richie. "We might need to dig up some sand."

"Here in the park?"

"Probably not," said Tommy. "I mean, if you were a Spanish conquistador back in the 1600s, would you hide your treasure chest in a state park?"

The ranger stared at Tommy. People do that sometimes.

"Are you folks looking for the lost pearl ship?" asked the ranger.

"Yes, indeed," said Uncle Richie. "But how on earth did you deduce that?"

The ranger shrugged. "Met an interesting fellow up at one of the resorts last night. We played a few hands of cards together—"

Uncle Richie's eyebrows went up. "Cards, you say?"

"Just a friendly game of hearts. We got to talking. He told me he had a treasure map. Said a strange and mysterious Native American lady just gave it to him because he's a well-known treasure hunter."

"Is that so?" I said. "Do you remember his name?"

"Dirk McDaniels."

We all nodded. Dirk McDaniels was new on the treasure-hunting circuit. But he looked good on TV. He did a lot of shows for the Exploration Channel.

"The mysterious woman promised Mr. McDaniels that the map would lead him straight to the lost ship of the desert—if he could decipher it. Of course, people have been saying that sort of thing around these parts for centuries..."

"Of course," said Uncle Richie. "Do you happen to recall where this intrepid gentleman, this Mr. McDaniels, was lodging?"

"About thirteen miles north of here. Place called the Borrego Springs Resort. It's a golfer's desert paradise."

"Is that so?" said Uncle Richie, acting interested.

"Yep," said the ranger. "I met McDaniels in their fireside lounge. It was prime rib Saturday."

"Sounds marvelous. Perhaps I will venture up that way this evening."

"You hoping he might share his treasure map with you?"

Uncle Richie grinned.

"Something like that."

So, later that night, Uncle Richie stuffed a deck of cards (his lucky ones, he told us) into his safari jacket and rode an ATV up to the resort to meet the map man.

Meanwhile, the rest of us kicked back, relaxed, and watched the incredible light show twinkling overhead. According to Storm, the nearby town of Borrego Springs was the first International Dark Sky Community in California.

"To cut down on light pollution, they restricted and modified the lights on public streets, outside businesses, and on people's porches. That's why we can see millions and millions of stars and even the murky swoosh of the Milky Way."

It was absolutely amazing. The most incredible night sky I've ever seen on dry land.

But our evening's celestial entertainment was interrupted by a video call from Mom and Dad.

The stars would have to wait.

CHAPTER 20

"How was your flight to California?" asked Mom.

"Awesome!" said Tommy.

The rest of us tried not to remember the landing. Or the barrel rolls. Or the loop-de-loops. Or whatever those other things were called when we were upside down and sideways with G-forces stretching our cheeks back to our ears.

"Did you enjoy that lunch I packed?" asked Dad.

Beck and I burped a little. We were remembering how we served up that lunch. Twice.

"We're safe on the ground," said Storm. "The stars in the desert are spectacular. We're enjoying our newfound freedom."

"Good," said Mom. "Where's Uncle Richie?"

"Off doing research," I told her.

"We have a lead on a pearl ship treasure map," added Beck.

"Your first day in the field?" said Dad. "I am impressed."

"Guess that's why Uncle Richie is such a treasure-hunting legend," said Tommy. Maybe because he hadn't heard Professor Hingleburt trash-talking Uncle Richie outside that bookshop. Or maybe because Uncle Richie let him land an airplane.

"How are things back in DC?" I asked.

"Very interesting," said Mom.

"Indeed," added Dad. "Do you kids remember Professor Hingleburt from that night in the Smithsonian?"

"Chya," said Tommy. "Cranky old dude needs to chillax."

"Be that as it may," said Dad, "it's possible

Professor Hingleburt and his associates have just made a remarkable discovery."

"If it's true," added Mom.

"What'd they find?" I asked.

"What they claim is one of the long-lost, handwritten, original copies of the Bill of Rights to the United States Constitution."

"Where'd they find it?" joked Tommy. "Kinko's?"

"Not exactly," said Mom. She shifted into history teacher mode. "You see, kids, in 1789, Congress agreed to draw up the Bill of Rights—the first ten amendments to the Constitution. George Washington, who, of course, was president at the time, directed three clerks to write out, by hand, fourteen copies of the bill. One was kept by the federal government. The others were sent to each of the thirteen original states for their ratification. However, some have been missing for years."

"What happened to them?" asked Beck.

"History suggests that Georgia's and New York's copies were likely burned," said Dad. "Georgia's during the Civil War and New York's during a fire at the state capitol in 1911. Pennsylvania's

I KNOW I PUT THAT DOCUMENT SOMEWHERE. PROBABLY SHOULD'VE SAVED iT ON MY LAPTOP.

copy was stolen in the late nineteenth century and Maryland is unsure of what happened to their copy."

"But here's the problem," said Mom. "The document Professor Hingleburt discovered in an old barn in western Maryland spells out very different rights than the text we're familiar with."

"How so?"

"The First Amendment," said Dad, "is almost the exact opposite of the one we all know and love."

"You mean..." I looked to Beck and we recited

it together fast, without taking a breath (it's another twin thing). "'Congress shall make no law respecting an establishment of religion, or prohibiting the free exercise thereof; or abridging the freedom of speech, or of the press; or the right of the people peaceably to assemble, and to petition the Government for a redress of grievances?'"

Mom nodded. "The First Amendment in Professor Hingleburt's newly discovered Bill of Rights says Congress *shall* make laws for all those things."

"We're certain it's a forgery," said Dad.

"It has to be," said Mom. "Otherwise, everything we've taught you guys about America and its freedoms will have been a lie!"

CHAPTER 21

"That's horrible," said Storm.

Dad nodded. "Fortunately, your mother is one of the foremost antiquarian handwriting experts in the world. We are insisting that she be given a chance to authenticate the document."

"Is Professor Hingleburt cooperating?" I asked.

"Not exactly," said Mom. "In fact, he suggested that the document in the National Archives is the forgery. That the founding fathers knew better than to give what he calls 'the ill-educated rabble' so much freedom. He thinks America might be stronger if people weren't allowed to say whatever they felt like saying whenever they felt like saying it."

"Ha!" Storm gave that a lip fart. Saying whatever she feels like saying (or lip farting) whenever she feels like doing it? That's how Storm rolls.

"Long story short," said Dad, "your mother and I are going to be quite busy here in DC."

"We were hoping to eventually join you kids and Uncle Richie on your treasure quest," added Mom. "But that's not going to work out. We'll be tied up for some time investigating this bogus Bill of Rights while simultaneously honoring our commitments at the Smithsonian."

"No worries," said Tommy. "Uncle Richie is cool. We're cool. Everything's cool."

We all nodded in agreement (even though three of us weren't so cool about Tommy flying Uncle Richie's plane).

"Good luck on your quest!" said Dad.

"Make us proud!" added Mom.

"Love you guys!" said Dad.

"Love you back!" we shouted in unison.

We signed off and were about to start gazing up at the stars again when Uncle Richie roared into our campsite on the ATV.

He was waving a rolled-up scroll of leather over his head.

"Eureka!" he shouted, as he fishtailed to a sand-spewing stop. "The map is ours!"

"Wha-hut?" said Beck. "Dirk McDaniels gave you the map?"

"Of course he did. Just as I would've given him one million dollars had the cards gone the other way."

"You wagered one million dollars?" I said. "In a card game?"

"Indeed, I did, Bick. We were playing war."

"So, uh, do you have a million dollars?" asked Beck.

"Of course not, Beck! But I knew I wouldn't need the money. For I held all the aces!"

"Did you find out anything about the mysterious woman who gave Mr. McDaniels the map?" asked Tommy.

"She didn't reveal her name or her identity," said Uncle Richie. "But Mr. McDaniels described her as a radiant princess with raven-black hair. A descendant of the Cahuilla tribe, which, of course, is native to this land. Just think—her people were sitting under this same blanket of stars long before Juan de Iturbe sailed up from Mexico, searching for precious pearls. They were also here when the Spaniard's great white bird flew up from Mexico."

In the still of the desert night, huddled around

the glowing embers of our flickering campfire, we were all mesmerized by the hypnotic sound of Uncle Richie's voice as he spun his tale. (The guy's an amazing storyteller. Even better than me.)

"You see, children, according to first peoples' legends, many years ago there were great floods in this desert. When this happened, the native people would climb to higher, drier land and live there until the water finally receded. One day, they saw a great big bird with many tall white wings come floating up on the floodwaters from down Mexico way."

"With time, the water went away but the bird was stuck in the sand. Its white wings fell away, leaving nothing but a skeleton of three tall and barren trees. The sand blew and blew, and, before long, the bird was completely covered up. She disappeared into the dunes."

"A great bird with tall white wings?" said Storm. "Three tall and barren trees? Sounds like a three-masted sailing ship to me."

Uncle Richie grinned. "Indeed. And the young lady's Cahuilla ancestors drew this map to commemorate exactly where that big bird is buried!"

CHAPTER 22

Uncle Richie unrolled the map, which was painted on a thin and crinkly animal hide.

Uncle Richie pointed a flashlight at a three-winged bird nestled between mountains or sand dunes.

"X marks the spot!" he proclaimed. "It lines up with legend. Notice the higher elevations. These mountains. That's where the wise Cahuilla people waited out the flood. Meanwhile, our seafaring friend, the poor pearl poacher Señor Juan de Iturbe, was trapped in the muck as the waters receded."

"Check out this pool of water with the crowd of people around it," said Beck, tapping an illustration. Uncle Richie swung his flashlight down to illuminate the spot.

"Is that a pair of palm trees?" asked Tommy, peering at the same detail.

"Dos Palmas," said Storm. "An artesian spring that was a watering place for Native Americans traveling across the Colorado Desert."

Uncle Richie nodded. "And, for many years, the palm-shrouded oasis at the foot of the mountains was also a spot to fill your canteens and water barrels as you made your way along the

Bradshaw Trail between San Bernardino and the gold mining boomtowns of Arizona."

Storm and Uncle Richie were definitely related. The guy could almost out-nerd her. They probably shared the same "obscure trivia" gene.

"But," said Storm, "Dos Palmas is located to the *east* of the Salton Sea, not the west as indicated on this primitive map."

"Maybe because compasses and directions hadn't been invented way back then," said Tommy.

"Or," suggested Beck, "maybe this is some kind of *secret* map. And you can only read it correctly if you know the code."

"Cool," said Tommy. "We've had secret maps before. Remember?"

"Totally," I said.

"Here's the key," said Storm, tapping the hummingbird icon in the corner of the map.

"Of course!" boomed Uncle Richie. "Well done, Storm! Ha! No wonder Dirk McDaniels thought this map was worthless. Laughed at me when I wagered a million dollars against it. Told me he's been following this map for weeks and found nothing but sand."

"Wait a second," said Tommy. "This map is no good?"

"Only if you don't know how to read it. Which, thanks to your genius sister Storm, we now do."

"Awesome!" I said. "So, uh, what did she just figure out?"

Uncle Richie turned to Storm. He was beaming. "Storm, if you please, enlighten us!"

"A hummingbird can fly backward," said Storm with a knowing smile.

"The map is backward," said Beck. "It's been flipped. To hide the secret!"

"Exactly!" said Uncle Richie. "We just need to flip everything around, orientating the map off the eastern shore of the Salton Sea. We also need to break camp at first light. Our treasure chest filled with black pearls awaits us in the desert sands north of Dos Palmas!"

CHAPTER 23

The next morning, while the sun was still rising, we quickly loaded up our gear. Beck and I would ride our ATVs behind the RV hauling the bulldozer.

We exited the park and swung north of the Salton Sea until we were headed east on the flat dirt of Box Canyon Road.

Until we saw the not-so-fun sinister black helicopter hovering overhead. It was tailing us!

I shielded my eyes from the scorching sun.

Looking up, I noticed a familiar logo painted on the belly of the black chopper chasing us up Box Canyon Road.

"NCTE!" I read out loud.

"Nathan Collier Treasure Extractors," Beck shouted back at me.

Nathan Collier was the biggest star on the Exploration Cable Channel. He was also the worst treasure hunter in the world. Collier would have a hard time finding the toy surprise hidden inside a box of Cracker Jack. That's why he was always following us Kidds around, hoping to snatch our finds out from under us or take credit for discoveries we'd already made.

And judging by his swooping chopper, Dirk McDaniels, the rising young star at the Exploration Channel, worked for NCTE. Nathan Collier was Dirk McDaniels's boss.

"Dirk McDaniels played Uncle Richie!" shouted Beck as we thundered up the dusty road.

I totally agreed with my twin sis. "McDaniels let Uncle Richie beat him in that card game so *we'd* decipher the map and lead him right to the ship. I'll bet he even sent that park ranger over to our campsite—to lure Uncle Richie to that bogus card game."

"We need to teach Collier and McDaniels a lesson!" said Beck.

"We sure do!"

I gunned my throttle and pulled up alongside the RV.

I could see Uncle Richie and Storm in the back, working on the computer in the galley.

I gave the ATV a little more gas and was riding parallel to Tommy, who was behind the wheel.

"Pull over!" I shouted at him.

"What? Who are you? The California Highway Patrol?"

"Pull over!" shouted Beck, who'd zoomed up on the other side of the RV.

Tommy eased off the gas and brought the lumbering vehicle to a stop.

The thumping helicopter hovered directly overhead.

Beck and I hopped off our ATVs and dashed into the RV.

"Why have we stopped?" asked Uncle Richie. "Do one of you children need to go to the potty? I'm told children need to do that on a frequent basis."

"We're being followed," I said, gesturing toward the ceiling. There was no mistaking the *whump-whump-whump* of the helicopter hanging in the air right above us.

"Who's in the chopper?" asked Tommy.

Beck turned to Uncle Richie. "Your buddy Dirk McDaniels."

"He works for Nathan Collier," I said.

"Collier!" said Tommy, pounding a fist into his palm.

"Ah," said Uncle Richie. "Your parents' number one nemesis."

"We think Mr. McDaniels let you win that map

on purpose," I said, "so *we'd* crack the code and lead him straight to the precious black pearls."

"It sounds like the sort of thing Collier and his cronies would do," added Storm.

"Then," said Uncle Richie, "we need to take them off our scent. Give them a red herring to chase, as it were." He looked at Tommy. "Thomas, you're about my size. Quickly now. We need to exchange outfits. You'll be me and I'll be you!"

CHAPTER 24

Tommy slipped into Uncle Richie's hat and safari jacket.

Uncle Richie borrowed Tommy's baseball cap.

"Take that road and lead them north on one of the ATVs, Thomas," Uncle Richie instructed. "Go as far as the Joshua Tree National Park, if need be. When you are in a remote enough location, pretend as if you are studying the treasure map and pacing off a goodly distance. Then start digging." He yanked a shovel out of the RV's utility closet.

"Um, wouldn't using the backhoe be faster?"

"Indeed. However, we will be employing it at the true dig site."

"Riiiiight."

"Plus, Thomas, you want to waste as much time and helicopter fuel as you can."

"Oh. Got it."

"Atta boy. Keep them distracted until they're flying on fumes. Eventually Mr. McDaniels and his chopper crew will head back to the Salton airfield to refuel. When they do, you can rejoin us at the true dig site."

"We'll text you the exact GPS coordinates," added Storm.

"Cool," said Tommy.

"Take this," said Uncle Richie, handing Tommy the rolled-up hide with the ancient backward map inscribed on it.

"Don't you guys need it?"

"Not anymore," said Storm. "We scanned it into the computer and matched it up with satellite imagery of the same area." She tapped her phone. A glowing map with a blinking green dot appeared on the screen.

"Awesome," said Tommy. "Anybody want a souvenir from Joshua Tree? Maybe a keychain or a snow globe?"

"A snow globe?" said Beck. "From the desert?"

"Good point. Catch you guys, later."

"One minute, Thomas," said Uncle Richie. "Time for some dramatic acting." He grabbed the RV's CB radio microphone. "Chances are, they will be monitoring all frequencies." He depressed the Talk button. "Breaker, breaker. This is Uncle Bear. Things are getting too risky out here in the sandbox. I'm leaving you children in the air-conditioned comfort of this lovely recreational vehicle where there is a bathroom and plenty of snacks. I, all by myself, shall head off to un-bury the treasure now that we know exactly where it is buried!"

He clipped the microphone back into its bracket.

"Good acting," said Tommy.

"Thank you. Whilst in London many years ago I took a few classes at the Royal Academy of Dramatic Arts. Now, Thomas, it's your turn. Be the best me that you can be."

"You got it!"

"Go!"

Tommy tugged down on Uncle Richie's Teddy Roosevelt hat, tucked the treasure map under his arm, grabbed the shovel, and raced out of the RV. He did his best to imitate Uncle Richie's brisk, arm-swinging gait and waved the map in the air so Dirk McDaniels could see it from his perch in the sky. He even said, "Bully! Bully!" a few times.

Tommy climbed aboard the nearest ATV, goosed the throttle, and blasted off—spewing rock chunks and careening up a rutted trail that would take him north and far, far away from where we were headed.

Dirk McDaniels and the NCTE whirlybird took the bait. They flew off after Tommy—the fake Uncle Richie.

"Bully!" said the real one when they were gone. "Let's give them at least a thirty-minute head start, shall we?" He pulled a deck of cards out of a side pocket in his cargo shorts. "Anyone interested in a friendly game of old maid?"

CHAPTER 25

Thirty minutes later, after we'd all lost our allowance money for the next ten years to Uncle Richie, we returned to our quest.

The map took us to a patch of sandy dunes nestled between two craggy mountain ridges.

Storm held her phone in her hand and marked off the last few paces to the spot where the ancient Cahuilla map showed the Lost Ship of the Desert to be buried.

Uncle Richie maneuvered the backhoe off its trailer and stationed its shovel teeth above a windswept crest in the sand. "And now we come to the critical moment in our grand adventure!"

he declared. "But remember, children, no matter what we might uncover here today, the only person who makes no mistakes is the one who never dares to do anything!"

And with that, he jimmied some levers and started scooping away the sand.

He gave us each a turn in the backhoe cab. In no time, we had shoveled out a hole that was twenty feet wide and twenty feet deep. We were far away from the nearest roadways. No one was there to see us do our digging, except for a few buzzards circling in the sky.

Beck was back in the cab for her second turn with the power shovel when we all heard something wooden crunch.

She'd hit the rotting timbers of the ship.

"Eureka!" shouted Uncle Richie. "You found it, Beck! Quickly now. To the RV. Everybody grab a broom, a brush, or a rake. It's time for the delicate work."

The four of us swept and whisked sand away for another hour. It was hard work because the wind kept working against us. But the shape of the ship (well, what was left of it) was slowly revealed inside the crater we'd carved into the desert.

"Here's the hatch for the cargo hold!" shouted Storm.

The rest of us raced over to join her. The rusty iron gate weighed a ton but, working together, we were able to pry it open.

Since we were the smallest, Beck and I each grabbed a flashlight and dropped down into the hold.

"See anything?" asked Uncle Richie, peering into the darkness where Beck and I had just bumped into something big and boxy.

"Nothing much," I said.

"Nothing at all," said Beck, playing along.

"Except for this old footlocker," I said.

"Or maybe it's, you know—a treasure chest!"

"Eureka!" cried Uncle Richie. "Well done, Bick and Beck. Well done, Storm."

"Well done to you, too!" I shouted. "You're the one who got us the treasure map."

"You're also the one who believed the crazy legend in the first place," added Beck.

"You guys?" said Storm. "Can we stop congratulating each other and extract the contents of the treasure chest? Tommy can't keep Dirk McDaniels and that helicopter distracted forever."

"Your sister is, of course, correct," said Uncle Richie. "We best save our celebratory festivities for another time and place. Are you two able to open the treasure chest? Do you need a pry bar?"

"Nope," I said. "There's no lock."

"Really?" said Uncle Richie, up on the deck. "Fascinating."

It took a few grunts, but Beck and I were able to heave open the creaky, squeaky lid. We swung our flashlights to inspect its contents.

We didn't see any precious black pearls. Or gold. Or jewels. Or bars of silver.

The big wooden box was practically empty.

The only thing inside the Lost Ship of the Desert's treasure chest was very weird and totally unexpected: a USB thumb drive.

CHAPTER 26

"**A** thumb drive?" said Uncle Richie after Beck and I climbed out of the hull of the shipwreck with our, uh, treasure.

"That's all that was in the chest," I told him.

"Except," added Beck, "for, you know, *sand!*"

Uncle Richie stroked his chin thoughtfully. "Indeed. Quite a bit of that in this location."

"Maybe somebody else found the treasure before we did," I said.

"It's a possibility," said Storm. "There are legends of a mule driver in the late eighteen-hundreds who came out of the desert, his saddle bags filled with riches."

"But what about the thumb drive?" I said. "Most mule drivers from the late eighteen-hundreds didn't carry those in their saddle bags."

"True," said Uncle Richie. "And they were hardly standard equipment on Spanish ships from the Age of Exploration."

"Because the first USB flash drive wasn't even sold in America until the year two thousand," said Storm. Yes, her brain is ginormous enough to remember just about anything, even stuff nobody really cares about.

I handed the flash drive to Uncle Richie, who tossed it up and down in his palm as if it were a peanut.

"I suspect there is only one thing for us to do," he said. "Storm? Will this work in your laptop?"

"Definitely."

"Bully. Contact Thomas. Instruct him to meet us at the Cottonwood Campground at the southern edge of the Joshua Tree National Park. We should all be together when these modern secrets of the Lost Ship of the Desert are revealed!"

Storm texted Tommy. We hitched the trailer

up to the RV and loaded the backhoe and remaining ATV. Rumbling across the rugged terrain, we found Box Canyon Road again and followed it until it crossed under an interstate and turned into Cottonwood Springs Road, which took us into the Joshua Tree National Park and its Cottonwood Campground.

Tommy was already there.

"I pretended like the treasure was buried up north, underneath one of the Joshua trees," he told us, swapping hats and vests with Uncle

Richie. "Dirk McDaniels watched me dig for about an hour and took off. His engine was kind of sputtering. I think he needed to go gas up."

"What'd you guys dig up?" Tommy asked.

Uncle Richie tossed him the flash drive. "Only this."

"Whoa. The Spanish Conquistadors had computers?"

"We think somebody else put it in the treasure chest," I said.

"Sometime after the year two thousand," added Storm.

"Cool," said Tommy. "Let's go check it out."

We all headed into the RV. Storm inserted the drive into a USB port on her laptop.

"It's a single document," said Storm after she clicked the file icon to open it.

What looked like a letter filled the screen.

"Uh-oh," I said. I recognized the big "E-1" logo in the letterhead. "It's from the Enlightened Ones."

All of a sudden, things had become much more mysterious.

CHAPTER 27

"**W**ho, pray tell, are these 'Enlightened Ones'?" asked Uncle Richie.

"A shadowy group of international art thieves," said Beck. "We've dealt with them before."

"Chya," said Tommy. "In Italy *and* Russia. E-1's totally twisted. They like to taunt treasure hunters. They'll give you clues because they get their kicks watching you try to figure 'em out."

"The Enlightened Ones," said Storm, "are also rumored to own the most spectacular collection of paintings, sculptures, and art treasures in the world. Typically, they don't purchase these masterpieces at art auctions. They steal them."

Uncle Richie nodded as he soaked in all the new information. "Read us what they say in their letter, Storm."

Storm scrolled down the page and started reading.

"'Congratulations, Mr. McDaniels.'"

"Mr. McDaniels?" said Uncle Richie. "Of course! They expected that Dirk McDaniels would be the one to unearth the Lost Ship of the Desert and discover its empty treasure chest. They didn't know he would wager his treasure map away in a friendly card game."

"Wait a second," said Tommy. "Do you think these Enlightened Dudes stole our precious black pearls?"

"Doubtful," said Storm. "They prefer priceless paintings and sculptures to rare gems. I suspect our friend the mule driver or an intrepid Native American made off with Señor Juan de Iturbe's cargo ages ago."

"Read on, Storm," said Uncle Richie. "This should prove most interesting."

Storm went back to reading: "'Congratulations,

Mr. McDaniels. You found the Lost Ship of the Desert quite handily. It took us more than a year, working with the very same Native American map, which we had in our warehouse of ancient etchings. You may very well be the intrepid treasure hunter we are seeking to help us find certain works of art that have, shall we say, gone missing. But before we back you with our unlimited financial resources for that ultimate quest, we require that you accept the challenge of a second test.'"

"A test?" said Tommy. "Like in school?"

"No," said Storm, who'd read ahead in the letter. "This will be another test of our treasure-hunting skills. Guess the Enlightened Ones wanted to make certain that Dirk McDaniels was super-skilled before they hired him to find whatever art they're looking for."

"This test might prove extremely dangerous," said Uncle Richie, probably because he was the adult in the room. "Perhaps we should simply quit while we're ahead and return to the safety and comfort of your parents' apartment in Washington, DC."

Storm shook her head. "Nope. We need to be in Virginia."

"Excuse me?"

"That's where we can hunt for another one of America's greatest missing treasures."

"Yes!" I said.

"Boo-yah!" added Beck.

Like Dad, Beck and I kept a list of real-life treasures still waiting to be found (preferably by us). A whole bunch were in America. Beale's missing millions, hidden somewhere in the Rocky Mountains. The Lost Dutchman Gold Mine in Arizona. The Lost Treasure of the Alamo. Gangster Dutch Schultz's Stash in the mountains of New York. Confederate Colonel John Singleton Mosby's Treasure in Virginia.

Virginia!

"Is it Mosby's treasure?" I blurted.

Storm nodded. "Yep. And there's another map with another code. Give me time, and I think I can crack it."

"Bully!" said Uncle Richie, eagerly rubbing his hands together. "Ah, Mosby's Raiders. I've been fascinated by their missing treasure for decades."

"Then let's go get it!" I said.

"We've got a map!" added Beck.

"And plenty of free time," said Tommy.

"I concur," said Storm.

"Shall we take a family vote?" suggested Uncle Richie. "All in favor of pulling up stakes and heading back east to search for Mosby's treasure in Virginia, kindly raise your right hand and say, 'Aye!'"

"Aye!" we all shouted.

"Any opposed?"

No one said "nay."

"Thomas?" said Uncle Richie. "Take the wheel. We need to return to the airport and fire up my plane. If we hope to find Mosby's treasure, we need to return to the other side of the continent."

"No problemo," said Tommy, slipping into the driver's seat. "So, who was this Mosby dude, anyway?"

"Storm? Would you like to do the honors?"

"No, thanks, Uncle Richie. I like the way you tell tales."

"Me, too," I said.

"Very well."

And while Tommy drove, Uncle Richie spun an amazing tale of action, adventure, and lost treasure.

He sort of reminded me of me.

CHAPTER 28

"**D**uring the Civil War, Confederate Colonel Mosby and his rebel riders made a daring night raid on the Fairfax County Courthouse, behind Union lines," said Uncle Richie as our RV hummed south on the interstate. "They captured forty-two Yankee soldiers without firing a single shot!"

"Whoa," said Tommy, behind the wheel.

"In the Union generals' room at the courthouse, they found gold, jewelry, candlesticks, and coins. Mosby and his men stuffed the treasure into a burlap sack, hopped on their horses, and headed back to the Confederate lines."

"But Mosby's raiders ran into a little bit of trouble on the ride home!" said Storm, picking up the thread.

"Indeed so," said Uncle Richie. "Their advance scouts came back with a dire warning: Mosby and his men were heading straight into a large group of Union soldiers. So, Mosby and his most trusted sergeant took the burlap sack filled with booty and buried it between two pine trees, both of which, legend has it, they marked with an X so they'd remember where they had buried their treasure.

"Months later, when they thought it would be safe, that sergeant and six of Mosby's best men rode back to recover the loot. But, before they could reach the secret location, they were captured by Yankees, and hanged outside Fort Royal in 1864. Mosby, himself, was never able to return to look for the treasure."

"So, it's still out there!" I said. "And we're gonna find it!"

"How much loot are we talking about?" asked Beck.

"Estimates put the value of the Civil War–era treasures at three hundred and fifty thousand dollars," said Storm. "Of course, those were 1864 dollars. Today, the treasure would be worth about five and a half million dollars!"

Tommy whistled.

"Children?" said Uncle Richie. "Let's go find those two pine trees in Fairfax County, Virginia!"

After stopping for some delicious In-N-Out

burgers (I got a Double-Double, fries, and a chocolate shake), we cruised into the Salton Sea Airport. It was nearly dusk. The air was cooling down. The sky darkening. I saw Uncle Richie's 1971 Piper Aztec airplane parked in front of a hangar where a mechanic in coveralls was wiping the sand off its windshield with a soiled cloth.

"Ah! Ms. Pamela Johnston! Finest aircraft mechanic in the contiguous United States!"

We pulled closer to the plane.

I thought Tommy's eyeballs were going to pop out of his head.

"You know her?" he asked. "That angel in the coveralls with the billowing blond hair wafting in the breeze? You actually know her?"

"Indeed, I do," said Uncle Richie. "She is a true friend to treasure hunters everywhere. She's the one who rented me all the gear we needed for our exploration."

"She's also beautiful," said Tommy. "I think I want to marry her."

Beck, Storm, and I rolled our eyes. *Here we go again.*

CHAPTER 29

"Hiya, Poppie," said the mechanic as she walked over to meet us. She tilted her head and gave us a wave.

"Greetings, Pamela," said Uncle Richie. "These are my fellow treasure hunters, the world-famous Kidd family. Bick, Beck, Storm, and Thomas. They are also my great-nieces and nephews."

"Howdy," said Ms. Johnston.

"Well, hello," said Tommy. "Are you a magician? Because when I look at you, everyone else disappears."

"Cute," said the mechanic, wiping her hands on a rag.

"Thanks," said Tommy. "I've been saving that one for a special occasion."

In the distance, I heard a familiar *whump-whump-whump.*

"Collier!" I said, pounding my fist into my open palm.

"You guys know Nathan?"

"We sure do," said Beck. She was about to spit on the ground when Pam the mechanic hit her with a follow-up.

"How about his new sidekick? Dirk McDaniels. Handsome, am I right, ladies?"

Storm snorted. Beck laughed.

"Is Nathan Collier Treasure Extractors using this airport, too?" I asked.

"Uh, yeah," said Pam. "It's the only one in the area."

"We mustn't let them spot us," said Uncle Richie. "Pamela, would you be so kind as to let us hide in your hangar?"

"Sure, Poppie. I'll put it on your tab." Along

with the equipment rentals.

"Our tab?" I said. "You'd charge us to hide in your hangar?"

She shrugged. "Girl has to make a living."

"Well that's the most—"

"Bick?" said Uncle Richie, shaking his head. The helicopter was approaching fast.

"The most ingenious thing I've ever heard."

"Quickly now," said Uncle Richie. "Into the hangar!"

We all rushed into another rusty Quonset hut and pulled the door tight behind us.

"When they land," said Ms. Johnston, "I'll go out and offer to refuel them. Help them tie down for the night."

"But you shan't tell them we are here?" said Uncle Richie.

"Of course not, Poppie. My silence is included in the Complete Hangar Hiding package."

"And how much does that cost?" asked Storm.

"Five hundred dollars," replied Ms. Johnston. "Per hour."

"You drive a hard bargain," said Uncle Richie. He held out his hand. The mechanic shook it. "Deal!"

She left. We took turns peeking through the grease-smeared window in the hut's door.

"That's Collier himself!" I said. "I'd recognize that oily spit curl on his forehead anywhere."

"McDaniels must've called for reinforcements after Tommy bluffed him into flying north," said Uncle Richie.

Collier and McDaniels were gesturing at Uncle Richie's twin-engine airplane. Ms. Johnston shrugged.

I got the feeling they were asking her about us and she was playing dumb, earning her $500 an hour.

Finally, McDaniels and Collier left the airfield.

"But," Ms. Johnston told us when she returned to the hangar, "they put a tracker on your plane."

"So?" said Tommy. "We can rip it off and bury it in the sand!"

"You do that, they'll know you were here and that I told you about the tracker. Collier might pay me more than five hundred dollars an hour to talk."

"But we need to fly to Virginia," I said.

"Really?" said Ms. Johnston, arching an interested eyebrow. "What's in Virginia?"

"Uh, our parents," said Beck. "Actually, they're in Washington, DC. But that's really close to Virginia."

"Well, you can't take your plane," said Ms. Johnston with a sly grin. "Not if you want to get the slip on Nathan Collier and Dirk McDaniels."

"Then how do you suggest we get there?" asked Uncle Richie, sounding like he already knew the answer.

"Simple, Poppie. Charter a private jet."

She gestured with her thumb over her shoulder. At a private jet. With AIR PAMELA painted on its side.

CHAPTER 30

Uncle Richie and his friend Ms. Johnston hammered out a deal.

"You can have thirty-three-and-a-third percent of whatever treasure we find in northern Virginia," he told her.

"Aha!" said Ms. Johnston. "I knew it! You guys are going on another treasure hunt!"

"Doh!" said Uncle Richie. "That was supposed to be a secret!"

Beck and I looked at each other. Maybe what Professor Hingleburt said about Uncle Richie outside that bookstore was true. Maybe he wasn't the sharpest treasure hunter in the toolshed.

"You have to keep it hush-hush," Tommy told her.

"Don't worry," she told him. "My lips are sealed."

"Oh. Too bad. It's a long flight. I was hoping to kill some time with some serious smooching..."

"Ewwwww!" Beck and I said at the same time.

"Can we hurry up and get out of here before I hurl my Double-Double?"

"Yes, indeed, Bick," said Uncle Richie. "Time is of the essence."

We loaded our duffel bags into the sleek jet.

"Can I help you fly it?" Tommy asked.

"No," said Ms. Johnston, totally shutting Tommy down.

"I've already done one landing—"

"No!"

I was starting to like Ms. Johnston more and more.

We took off a little before midnight. Ms. Johnston's fancy little jet had wi-fi so we were able to do an early morning video call with Mom and Dad back east.

We didn't tell them anything about Nathan Collier or the Enlightened Ones. We figured they had enough to worry about back in Washington. Turns out we were right.

"Dr. Hingleburt found another lost copy of the Bill of Rights," said Mom, sounding skeptical. "The First Amendment reads the same way as the first one he found."

"Implying," said Dad, "that Congress *should* make laws limiting the freedoms of speech, religion, and assembly."

"Have you studied the document?" asked Storm.

"Yes," said Mom. "Professor Hingleburt finally allowed a few of us to spend thirty minutes with the first document he discovered. If it is a forgery, it's a darn good one!"

"To make matters worse," said Dad, "he's been all over TV, telling whoever will listen that, 'It's time for a new America! The true America. One founded on the founding fathers' visionary curbs on freedoms!'"

"No one's listening to him, though," I said. "Are they?"

Mom and Dad both sighed.

"They're starting to," said Mom.

"And this discovery of a second identical document is lending credence to Professor Hingleburt's claim that the Bill of Rights enshrined in the National Archives is the true forgery."

After that, the rest of the flight across America was kind of quiet.

"I wish we could help Mom and Dad," Beck whispered to me.

"Yeah. Me, too."

Unfortunately, we couldn't. Unless, of course, we could dig up another one of the missing copies of the Bill of Rights. Maybe Colonel Mosby had stolen one of those, too.

When we landed in northern Virginia (smoothly—Tommy was snoozing in the copilot seat at the time), a strange, computerized voice that sounded like it gargled with gravel started talking to us through the ceiling speakers. It wasn't our pilot, Ms. Johnston.

It was one of the Enlightened Ones.

PART II

DIGGING
DEEPER

CHAPTER 31

"**C**ongratulations, whoever you are," said the deep and creepy voice. "We know that, somehow, you bested Dirk McDaniels and his colleagues in the quest to find the Lost Ship of the Desert. We also know that you have taken up our challenge and embarked on your second test: finding Mosby's treasure."

"How do they know that?" I asked.

"They have spies everywhere," said Beck. "Remember?"

"Be advised," said the computer-altered voice,

"this time you are searching for something that we, ourselves, could not find. The coded clue in the document will take you only as far as we were able to proceed. Finding the buried treasure? That will be up to you. If you successfully locate it, kindly text photographic evidence to the number noted in the thumb drive file. Once you do, we will contact you again with further instructions."

"Can we talk back to this Darth Vader dude?" asked Tommy, rubbing his fingertips along the ribbed speaker in the ceiling, looking for some kind of switch to flick.

"Since you cannot talk back or ask questions of me at this time…"

"Bummer," mumbled Tommy.

"…I will attempt to answer the question you are most likely asking: What's in this game for you? Why should you keep finding these hard-to-find treasures for us?"

"Exactly!" said Tommy, tossing up his arms. "You read my mind, bro."

"Complete these tasks and you will prove to us that you are, indeed, the finest treasure hunters in all of America."

"Not to mention the world!" added Tommy.

"Pass these tests, and we will immediately offer you an opportunity to earn twenty million dollars. Happy treasure hunting. We hope to hear from you again, soon. Whoever you are."

"I'm Tommy," said Tommy. "Tommy Kidd."

"Um, they can't hear you," I reminded him.

"Interesting," said Uncle Richie, rubbing his chin thoughtfully. I figured he was imagining all the card games he could enter with his share of twenty million dollars.

"What's one third of twenty million, Poppie?" said Ms. Johnston as she steered the jet off the active runway.

"I believe our deal was for whatever treasure we found here in northern Virginia, Pamela."

"Well, we're in northern Virginia. And this new treasure just found you. I'm tagging along for the full ride."

"Fine by me," said Tommy, wiggling his eyebrows.

"You guys?" I said. "The twenty-million-dollar deal only happens *after* we find Mosby's treasure."

"Bick's right," said Beck. "We need to stay focused."

"Which I have been doing this entire flight," said Storm.

I noticed she had several paper coffee cups stacked up inside each other in her seatback pocket. I don't think she slept a wink on the whole five-hour flight from California.

"I figured out the clue in the document. It tells us where we need to go next."

"Where?" asked Tommy.

"Dixie Dipper Frozen Treats. An ice cream place."

"Huh?" I said.

"That's kind of random," added Beck, raising an eyebrow.

Storm shrugged. "Sorry. But that was the answer to the substitution cipher in the E-1 document that I have been working on for the past five hours. To crack it, I realized I needed to add up the numerals in the phone number they want us to text if we should prove successful, then divide the number of digits in that number by ten. The answer told me how many letters I needed to skip forward in the alphabet to find the coded letters' replacements."

Dumbfounded, the rest of us just nodded. Very, very slowly.

"So, uh, where is this Dixie Dipper Frozen Treats?" I asked.

"At the intersection of Routes Twenty-nine and Two-eleven in Warrenton, Virginia," said Storm. "Right in the heart of Mosby's Raiders' territory."

CHAPTER 32

We rented a van at the airport and set off for Warrenton, Virginia.

We also stopped off at a home supply store to pick up a pair of shovels and one of those rock-prying bars. We Kidds are like the Boy Scouts. "Be prepared" is our family motto.

"Warrenton is very close to where many suspect Mosby hid his treasure," said Storm.

"Now we just need to find two really tall pine trees marked with Xs near this Dixie Dipper Frozen Treats place," I said.

"So, what do you think we should do, Bickford?"

said Beck. "Hike through the forest, looking for trees?"

"Not just trees, Rebecca—pine trees!"

Yep. You guessed it. Groggy from our transcontinental flight, we exploded into Twin Tirade 2003.

"Oh, that narrows it down!" said Beck.

"It definitely does!" I told her. "Pine trees are easy to spot."

"So are lamebrains like you!"

"Pine trees are evergreens, sis. That means they're always green!"

"Just like your breath and your boogers."

"My breath isn't green!"

"No, it's just toxic. Like swamp gas."

Ms. Johnston was gawking at us. She'd never witnessed a twin tirade before.

"Give 'em a minute," said Tommy from behind the wheel. "It'll blow over."

"Hey, what color is swamp gas?" I asked.

"Don't know. But there's a library." Beck pointed out the window at the Warrenton Branch of the Fauquier County Public Library we'd just passed. "They'd know."

"They might also know something about Mosby's treasure."

"Librarians know everything."

"And, even if they don't, they know how to find it."

"Good point, Bick."

"Thanks, Beck."

And that's how we ended up in the library, talking to Barbara Rhodes, a research librarian who'd grown up in the area and knew all the Mosby legends. We spent the whole afternoon with her.

She showed us all sorts of maps and old photographs.

THE ONLY THING WE DIDN'T FIND IN THE LIBRARY?
A TREASURE MAP!

"Oh, there are so many stories about where that burlap sack is buried," Ms. Rhodes told us after we'd been doing research together for almost eight hours. "But, the one I like best, probably because I live here in Warrenton, is that the hiding place is right up the road, at the intersection of Routes Twenty-nine and Two-eleven."

"Um, isn't that where the Dixie Dipper Frozen Treat stand is located?" I asked.

The librarian smiled and nodded.

"Do you think it's, like, buried in their basement?" asked Tommy.

"That's always been my hunch."

"So why haven't you tried digging it up?" asked Beck.

"Can't say for sure. Maybe because, for me, the legend is more precious than any treasure. If we find Colonel Mosby's buried burlap sack, the story's over."

True, I thought, *but we'd also be one step closer to twenty million dollars!*

We took pictures of some of the photos and copied several of the maps.

"We can't thank you enough for your kind assistance," Uncle Richie told Ms. Rhodes. Then he doffed his hat like a prince would and kissed her hand. "If there is ever anything I can do for you, please do not hesitate to call."

He handed her a crisp business card.

Ms. Rhodes tittered.

Tommy whipped out his phone and recorded a voice memo. "Note to self. Order business cards to hand out to the ladies."

It was dark when we left the library. Brain-dead from all those hours in the stacks, we decided to head to Dixie Dipper for some dessert.

And maybe we'd check out their basement, too.

CHAPTER 33

"**W**here you folks from?" asked the gangly guy behind the cash register as he rang up our ice cream cones.

(I got soft serve vanilla dipped in chocolate. Delish.)

"Oh, all over," replied Uncle Richie, very grandly. "For you see, good sir, we are treasure hunters!"

"Is that so?"

"Indeed, it is."

"Find anything interesting lately?"

"Uh, yeah," said Tommy. "You ever heard of the Lost Ship of the Desert?"

"There was a ship?" said the cashier. "In the desert?"

"It was lost," said Beck.

"But then," said Tommy, "we found, like, this treasure map, and—*boom!*—there it was, buried in the sand."

"You folks down here looking for Mosby's treasure?"

"Maybe," said Beck. "We usually don't talk about our quests until they're complete."

"Oh, dear," said Uncle Richie. "My great-niece is correct. Good sir? Kindly disregard anything I said about treasure or the hunting of it."

"No problem. But, if you folks are fans of the Mosby legends, check out our walls. We've got all sorts of memorabilia hanging on them. Including a few pages from Colonel Mosby's private journal."

"Bully!" said Uncle Richie.

"Do you also have a basement?" I asked.

"No," said the cashier. "And the next time you see Ms. Rhodes over at the library, kindly ask her to stop telling people that we do! Next!"

We moved into the dining room so the cashier

could ring up other customers.

"Here is his handwritten journal," said Storm, pointing to a frame displaying two scraps of antique parchment.

"Cool," I said. "If only he'd written down instructions about where he hid his loot."

Storm leaned in and peered at the two pages. One was completely covered in inky scribblings. The other page was half empty.

MOSBY'S CIVIL WAR DIARY

Storm tapped the glass on the frame. The side without any writing.

"Maybe he did leave us instructions," she whispered. "Uncle Richie?"

"Yes, Storm?"

"Could you please go back to the counter and order a cup of tea? Maybe a grilled cheese sandwich? Some hot soup would be good, too."

"Hungry, eh?"

"Nope."

She tapped the glass again. "See that F?"

We all leaned in and peered at the ancient paper. There was a tiny *F* inked into the corner.

"What does it mean?" asked Ms. Johnston.

"That there's something on this paper written in invisible ink," Storm whispered. "It's an old code from the Revolutionary War. British spies used to mark their dispatches written in invisible ink with a F for flame or an A for acid. If you heat this document with a flame, stuff written in invisible ink will appear on the paper. We don't have a candle to hold up to this glass, but maybe some steaming hot food will do the trick."

We all raced back to the counter and ordered one of every steaming item they had on the menu, along with several cups of coffee, tea, and cocoa. Then we all huddled around the framed document, warming it with our food and drinks.

Storm was right.

Slowly, lines that had been penned in invisible ink started to appear on the blank half of the second sheet of paper until they revealed a map.

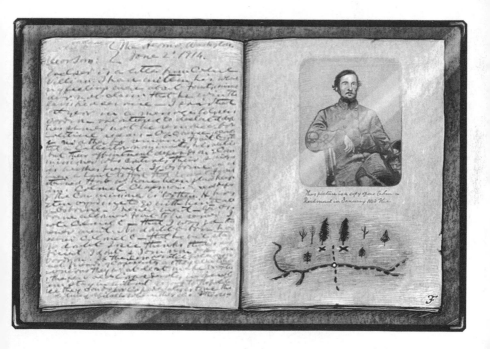

One that led from a crossroads, into the forest, and two trees marked with Xs.

Mosby's long-lost treasure was about to be found!

CHAPTER 34

W e hurried out of the ice cream shop and grabbed the shovels and rock-prying bar out of our van.

"Lead on, Storm!" cried Uncle Richie. "Lead on!"

"Yeah," said Ms. Johnston. "Show me the money!"

Storm pointed toward the intersection. "When the light changes, we need to cross that highway and cut through the Wawa parking lot."

Wawa, in case you didn't know, is a convenience store, like a 7-Eleven. So far, this was probably the weirdest, most suburban treasure hunt we'd ever been on.

"Cut through these trees," said Storm, indicating a tidy clump at the edge of the Wawa parking lot. "This way."

She, of course, had memorized the treasure map. She'd just scanned it into her hard drive, the same way a computer would. It really is incredible the way Storm's mind works sometimes.

"This used to be a forest," she remarked, as we hiked through several well-manicured backyards, toting our digging tools, looking like grave robbers.

Tommy banged the pry bar against a swing set. "Oops. Sorry about that."

"Shhhh!" whispered Uncle Richie. "Stealth and silence are essential to a mission such as ours, Thomas!"

"Right. Gotcha. My bad. But, in my defense, I didn't see the swing set and—"

"Shhhh!" We all said it. Even Ms. Johnston.

Storm gave us a series of intricate hand signal directions, the kind we do when we're diving. We needed to head into a thick grove of dark trees.

We crunched into what was starting to feel like an undeveloped section of forest.

"This is probably exactly how it was during the Civil War!" I said out loud, because we had moved far enough away from any homes.

"Indeed," said Uncle Richie. "One can easily imagine Mosby and his raiders riding across this very same ground on horseback."

Tommy started sniffing. "I can even smell the horse poop," he said.

"From the Civil War?" said Beck.

"No," said Tommy, examining the bottom of his shoe. "I think this is fresh."

Suddenly, I heard a distant howl of a blood-hound.

"You guys?" I said. "Do you think we're being followed?"

"That was just a dog, Bick," said Beck. "A lot of people in the suburbs have dogs."

"How much farther, Storm?" asked Uncle Richie, sounding eager to end our adventure in the deep woods, even if the howling was only coming from a beagle in its backyard.

"It should be somewhere right around here," said Storm.

"Fan out, children," said Uncle Richie. "Remember: We are looking for a pair of pine trees marked with Xs!"

"Wouldn't they have disappeared by now?" asked Beck.

"The actual marks, perhaps. Their scars? Never. Look for any unnaturally crisscrossing lumps or bumps in the bark."

"Just the pine trees, though, right?" said Tommy.

"Correct."

We spread out, miniature flashlights swinging.

I started rubbing pine trees. My fingers got sticky from sap.

But I didn't feel any Xs on any trees.

Just one short, bumpy gash, swollen over with a mound of bark. It was a huge evergreen tree. Like it might've been standing there for more than a century.

It was ten feet away from another towering giant.

I went over to examine its bark.

And saw another lumpy gash.

"You guys?" I called out. "I might've found something. Here. And over there!"

"Bully!" shouted Uncle Richie. He came running over, his flashlight bobbing with every stride. The others came bounding over, too. Everybody's beams of light started flying up and down the bark of the twin pines.

"Um, I don't see one X," said Beck. "Let alone two!"

I grinned. "Maybe we're not supposed to be looking for an X mark," I said.

"What are you suggesting, Bick?" said Uncle Richie, with a twinkle in his eye.

"That what we're really supposed to be looking for is…"

I waited, just to build up the suspense. It's fun to do sometimes. Especially in the middle of a dark forest in the middle of the night.

"What?" said Beck, who's not big on suspense. "What are we supposed to be looking for?"

I couldn't torture them any longer.

"A pair of *ax* marks. Not X marks. *Ax* marks." I pointed to the two trees. "Like those right there."

CHAPTER 35

"**E**ureka!" cried Uncle Richie. "Well done, Bick! We need to start digging!"

"Where?" asked Tommy eagerly.

"We'll burrow out a trench between these two pines. Break up the roots and rocks with the pry bar, Tommy. Bick and Beck? You handle the first shift on the shovels."

"Good idea," said Storm. She's not big on manual labor. Prefers brain work to brawn work.

Tommy pried out the rocks and roots. Beck and I dug. And dug.

Those hounds in the distance? That's right—
the howling had gone plural. Plus, they sounded
closer, too.

After thirty minutes, Tommy and Uncle Richie
took over on the digging. Beck and I took turns
slamming the pry bar. Ms. Johnston cheered us
on. Storm worked on her pine cone collection.

Thirty more minutes passed. Beck and I were
back on shovel duty. Ms. Johnston had started

breaking rocks. Uncle Richie and Tommy were squeezing the sweat out of their shirts. Storm was stacking her pine cones into a pretty nifty-looking pyramid.

Our trench was ten feet long, three feet deep, and, so far, empty. Except for rocks and roots and a rusty soda pop can from the late 1980s.

"Maybe Bick was wrong," suggested Storm. "Maybe those weren't the two trees."

"Chya," said Tommy. "Although all this shoveling and pry bar slamming has totally pumped up my guns." He flexed his arm muscles for Ms. Johnston.

She rolled her eyes.

I scooped up another load of dirt.

And the next time I sank my shovel into the ground, I felt something softy and mushy rip open.

Then I heard a *clink, clink, tinkle, tinkle.*

The kind of sound gold coins make when they tumble out of a torn burlap sack that's been rotting in the ground for more than a hundred years.

Beck and I dropped to our knees and scraped away more dirt by hand. Pretty soon, we saw it all: gold coins, jewelry, fancy candlesticks, silverware (the kind made out of real silver).

"It's Mosby's treasure!" shouted Beck. "Quick! Someone take a picture! The Enlightened Ones wanted photographic evidence of our treasure find."

Tommy knelt down and snapped several photos. Then he grabbed a couple thumbs-up selfies with the pile of pirate booty in the background.

"How much gold is that?" asked Ms. Johnston, grabbing a snapshot with her cell phone, too.

"A ton!" I said.

Storm quickly corrected me. "That doesn't look like two thousand pounds of gold and merchandise, Bick."

"Well, you said all this stuff was worth three hundred and fifty thousand dollars back in the day, which would be five and a half million dollars today! If you ask me, that's a ton!"

Uncle Richie scooped up a handful of coins and examined them.

"Ah! 1861 Liberty Head Double Eagles," he said. "Minted with gold from the California gold rush. Each coin was worth twenty dollars at the dawn of the civil war. Now you could melt one down and sell its gold for more than a thousand dollars. Or, you could sell it to a collector for ten times that amount. But nothing is more valuable than this lovely lady circled by thirteen stars. Miss Liberty, herself. She is what the boys in blue were fighting for. Liberty! Freedom! America!"

Ms. Johnston applauded slowly. "Nice speech, Poppie," she said. "But don't forget our deal. I'm still selling my third of all that loot."

"As you wish, Pamela. As you wish. It's just

that, sometimes, we true treasure hunters are momentarily overwhelmed by the historical—"

He didn't get to finish that thought.

In all the excitement about digging up the buried treasure, we'd sort of stopped paying attention to all those sounds in the distance.

Like the baying of bloodhounds.

And now the pounding of horse hooves.

It was like a nighttime foxhunt was underway in the forests of Virginia.

And we were the foxes they were hunting.

CHAPTER 36

The hounds arrived at our treasure ditch first. They were yapping and barking and woofing like crazy.

The horses and riders showed up like ten seconds later. There were four of them carrying torches, decked out in Confederate cavalry uniforms—and looking extremely scary.

Except the leader.

I'm sorry. The guy was maybe five feet tall and nearly bounced out of his saddle when the horses came galloping through the trees. He was also wearing the red jacket, white pants, and tiny black helmet that foxhunters wear in oil paintings.

"Whoa!" the leader of the night riders cried out, tugging back hard on his reins. "I said, 'Whoa!' Stop! Quit walking, horse!"

The horse ignored him and started prancing around in circles while making slobbery lip fart noises and flapping its flyswatter of a tail.

One of the other raiders reached over and yanked back on the leader's reins, trying to settle the boss's horse. But when he leaned in, he dipped his flaming torch right in front of the horse's face, which spooked that horse, which spooked all of the other horses.

"Are you an idiot, Beauregard?" shouted the tiny leader, hanging on to his helmet, as his frightened steed tried to buck him out of the saddle. "How much am I paying you idiots?"

"Who you callin' an idiot?" said the night rider, twirling his torch menacingly, which spooked the horses even more.

"Stand back, everybody," advised Uncle Richie. "This might be the gentleman in red's first pony ride."

As the horses bucked, all the torches started bobbing up and down, creating quite a fiery light show, which none of the horses seemed to be enjoying. They reared up on their hind legs. They kicked with their front hooves. They neighed in terror.

And that made the dogs start howling, which scared the horses even more.

I looked at Beck. She looked at me. We both shook our heads.

We've encountered a lot of bad guys on our treasure-hunting adventures. So far, these guys were the lamest.

While the riders coaxed their horses, Tommy tried, nonchalantly, to block everybody's view of our unburied treasure, sitting right there, scattered in the ditch.

"Easy, boy!" said the leader.

"That's a girl, sir," said one of his riders.

"Easy, girl!" said the leader.

"Might I suggest you douse your torches?" said Uncle Richie, trying to be helpful. "Horses don't like fire."

"Neither do we," said Storm.

"Fine. Whatever," said the leader. "Dump the torches in the ditch, you idiots."

Torches were tossed into our pit. Before they extinguished themselves, they cast a flickering orange light on our glittering pile of gold and silver.

"Well, well, well," said the leader, smiling smugly. "Would you look at that? I believe you interlopers have uncovered my treasure for me."

"Excuse me?" said Storm. "What makes you think any of our backbreaking manual labor was done for you?"

"Allow me to introduce myself," said the little man, sliding sideways in his saddle and easing himself, slowly, to the ground. When he finally did, he adjusted all his fancy riding clothes to make certain they still looked fancy. "My name is Milton T. Mosby, formerly from Minnetonka, Minnesota."

"Mosby?" I said. "Like in 'Mosby's Raiders'?"

"That's right, little man. Colonel John Mosby was my great-great-great-great-great-great uncle. And that treasure down there? That's *Mosby's* treasure. That means it's mine!"

CHAPTER 37

"**I** beg to differ with you, good sir," said Uncle Richie. "We are the ones who followed the clues, which led to the treasure map, which led us to this spot between two pine trees."

"Well," said Milton Mosby, "I guess I'm just smarter than you idiots. I skipped the first two parts—the annoying bit with the clues and the map—and just followed you. It was a whole lot easier." He tapped his temple. "Like I said, I'm a whole lot smarter than any of you will ever be."

"Ha," said Storm. "Prove it."

She immediately launched into a classic brain teaser.

"There are three houses. One is red, one is blue, and one is white. If the red house is to the left of the house in the middle, and the blue house is to the right of the house in the middle, where is the white house?"

"Easy," scoffed Milton Mosby. "In the middle."

"No," said Storm. "The White House is in Washington, DC."

She held up her right palm. I slapped her a high five. Beck slapped her five downtown on the left.

Mosby fumed.

"I'm also a multibillionaire!" he shouted.

"Congratulations, sir," said Ms. Johnston, with a sweet smile. The lady seemed to be super-interested in money.

"Thank you. I give away a good deal of money to charity and scholarly research."

"How about Most Humble Man in the World?" asked Beck. "Is that you, too?"

"Not sure. The voting isn't until next month. But, fingers crossed."

"If I may," said Uncle Richie, "how did you

even know we would be on a treasure hunt in this neck of the woods this evening?"

"Easy. Smart, rich people like me pay poor, simpering idiots like that skinny kid with the pimples at the ice cream parlor to text them anytime people seem more interested in Mosby's Treasure than Moose Tracks, Rocky Road, or salted caramel."

He jabbed a thumb over his soldiers at the riders dressed up like Rebel Raiders. "I keep these scary gentlemen with torches and horses on retainer."

One of the riders shrugged. "It's just a hobby."

"We're Civil War reenactors," said another one.

"I need to get my uniform dry cleaned," said a third, wiping stringy horse slobber off his pants leg. "Again."

Milton T. Mosby marched over to Uncle Richie like a preening peacock.

"Wait a second," said Mosby. "You're Richie 'Poppie' Luccio. I've heard about you. You're a famous, or should I say, *infamous* treasure hunter. Dr. Hingleburt, whose brilliant research

I support with beaucoup bucks, told me your sad tale. Something about a treasure you donated to a museum in Australia but then you took it all back because you admitted it was fake and you were a fraud. That's you, am I right?"

"Yes," said Uncle Richie, smiling gamely. "I suppose it is."

"Well, don't worry. You won't have to donate this treasure to a museum and then ask for it back because, guess what? I'm taking it all."

"I'd like to see you try," said Tommy, stepping forward bravely.

"Careful, sonny boy. My men have weapons."

"Aw, they're just fakes," said one of the Civil War reenactors, pulling out his pistol.

"Mine fires blanks," said another.

"Mine's made out of wood," said the third. "Whittled it myself."

"Well," cried Milton T. Mosby, brandishing a very nasty, very modern-looking handgun. "My revolver is real!"

"Show him your weapon, Poppie!" said Ms. Johnston.

"Actually," said Uncle Richie, "I never carry weaponry. Never saw the point of it."

Until now, I wanted to say, but didn't. Uncle Richie looked embarrassed enough.

So, we all held up our hands—including the three Civil War reenactors—while Milton T. Mosby scampered into the ditch with one hand aiming his pistol, the other one scooping up all of what used to be *our* treasure.

CHAPTER 38

Mr. Mosby stuffed all the treasure into a duffel bag.

"This comes at a most convenient time," he said. "Dr. Hingleburt needs more financing for his research into the original Bill of Rights."

He tapped an app on his phone.

"My car will be here in five," he said, keeping his pistol up. "No way am I riding that crazy horse out of here. Gentlemen? For services rendered."

He tossed a gold coin to one of the mounted Civil War reenactors who snatched it in midair.

"What's this for?" the guy asked.

"Your payment, idiot!"

The guy side-armed the coin back at Mosby and dinged him in his riding helmet.

"Don't want it," he said. "That treasure ought to go into a museum or something."

"Hear, hear," said Uncle Richie.

"Fine," said Mosby, pocketing the gold coin. "More for me to donate to Dr. Hingleburt."

He looked at Tommy, Storm, Beck, and me.

"Wait a second. If he's Richie Luccio, you four must be the Kidd brats."

"We prefer 'the Kidd kids,'" I said. "It has a certain zing to it."

"This old fool is your great-uncle!" laughed Mr. Mosby. "And your mother is the one giving the good professor, Dr. Hingleburt, so much grief about his incredible new finds."

"That's my niece," said Uncle Richie, proudly. "Susan Luccio Kidd. Smartest kid in her class, from kindergarten to graduate school."

"Only because she never had a class with me!" bragged the little blowhard. "And, if she's so smart, tell her to back off. There's a new America dawning. She could get hurt, sticking her nose where it doesn't belong."

"Oh, I don't tell Susan anything," said Uncle Richie, smiling broadly. "She can handle herself quite well without any assistance from me. Why, I remember this one time, when she was only six years old, we were together in the land formerly known as Persia, searching for Ganj-e Bada-vard—'the treasure brought by the wind'—which, of course, was the name of one of the legendary eight treasures of the Sasanian king Khosrow II..."

Uncle Richie didn't get to finish that story.

A rumbling SUV came crashing through the forest.

"So long, fools!" said Mr. Mosby. "My ride is here."

"Is that an Uber?" I asked. Because I had to.

"Ha! Uber is for ordinary people. And, as you know, I am extraordinary! This is a Suber-Duber! They'll pick you up anywhere, even in the woods."

Milton T. Mosby tossed his duffel into the backseat of the SUV, climbed in, and took off.

"You folks want us to chase after him?" asked one of the reenactors on horseback.

"We could turn him over to the police," said another.

"We know the sheriff," said the third.

"No need," said Ms. Johnston, sort of surprising the rest of us. "Let him enjoy his treasure. It's small potatoes."

"Small potatoes?" I said.

"Hello?" said Beck. "Earth to private jet lady. That loot is worth millions!"

"Five and a half million dollars, to be precise," I reminded everybody.

The three horsemen whistled.

Ms. Johnston grinned. "Like I said, small potatoes." She turned to the reenactors. "Good night, gentlemen. I would suggest you not answer any more of Mr. Mosby's phone calls."

"Yes, ma'am," said one. "We're sorry for any inconvenience and loss of treasure we may have caused you and your friends. Y'all have a good rest of your night."

The three men rode off into the Virginia night.

Ms. Johnston waited to make certain they were far enough away that they wouldn't hear what she said next.

"This is our lucky day!" she finally announced.

"Seriously?" I said. "We just found one of the long-lost American treasures..."

"And then we lost it," said Beck.

"My lucky day was when I met you," said Tommy, trying his best to get his groove thing going.

Ms. Johnston ignored him. Again.

"That bag full of coins and candlesticks is practically worthless compared to your next assignment," Ms. Johnston said with a laugh.

"Assignment?" I said. "What is this? School? Treasure Hunting 101?"

"No. I texted a photo of our find to the Enlightened Ones the minute you dug it up. They were mightily impressed. They want your help recovering one more lost treasure. Find it, and the twenty-million-dollar recovery fee will be yours. Except, of course, for one third of it, which will be mine!"

CHAPTER 39

"You sent them photographic evidence of our discovery?" Uncle Richie asked Ms. Johnston. "Already?"

She nodded.

"I was going to send them one of my selfies," said Tommy, pouting a little.

"Time is of the essence!" said Ms. Johnston. "Besides, reporting on your treasure-hunting capabilities is what they hired me to do."

"Excuse me?" said Beck.

"Yeah," I said, "excuse me, too. You're working for the Enlightened Ones?"

Ms. Johnston shot me a wink. "I'll work for anybody who pays well and on time."

"So," said Uncle Richie, "that's why Nathan Collier was using your airport facility services as well?"

"You guessed it, Poppie. He was in the running for this gig, too. But you guys totally knocked Collier and that newbie Dirk McDaniels out of the competition with your Lost Ship of the Desert score. Then you dig up Mosby's treasure? Poppie, I've got to tell you. Even I'm impressed."

Uncle Richie gave her a look like he wished she would quit calling him by his nickname. "Poppie" was what his friends called him. I had a feeling that Ms. Johnston wasn't a friend anymore. She was just a mercenary, selling out to the highest bidder.

"So, what's our new assignment?" I asked. "What do the Enlightened Ones want us to find for them next? A needle in a haystack?"

"A polar bear in a snowstorm?" said Beck.

"Waldo?" said Tommy.

"How about a priceless piece of missing or stolen art?" asked Storm.

"Bingo!" said Ms. Johnston.

Storm just shrugged. "We've dealt with these E-Ones before. They're art buffs. They like adding to their private collection—especially if it's a priceless painting that has fallen off the face of the earth, preferably through theft."

"Well, this one fits the bill," said Ms. Johnston.

"Um, can we talk about this somewhere besides the deep woods?" I said, swatting the back of my knee. "I think my bug spray is wearing off."

So we hiked back to the Dixie Dipper.

The gangly guy wasn't working behind the counter anymore.

"A customer pulled into the drive-thru and gave him a solid-gold coin as a tip," explained the girl who had taken his place. "I wish somebody would give me a solid-gold coin. All I ever get in my tip cup are quarters, nickels, and dimes."

We ordered some snacks and beverages, tipped her with several dollar bills, and headed back to the van for a meeting.

"Very well, Pamela," said Uncle Richie, slurping

on his milkshake, "tell us what missing American treasure we will be hunting down next for your mysterious friends."

"It could be your most difficult quest ever," said Ms. Johnston.

"Doubtful," said Storm. "But do go on."

"Are you familiar with Vermeer's painting *The Concert*?" she asked.

The rest of us turned to Storm.

She did not disappoint.

"Vermeer's *The Concert* is considered to be the most valuable stolen painting in the world," she replied. "It was taken as part of the largest art heist in history, which took place on March 18, 1990, when two thieves disguised as police officers stole thirteen pieces of art from the Isabella Stewart Gardner Museum in Boston. The combined worth of all the art stolen that one night is estimated to be five hundred million dollars. None of it has ever been recovered."

CHAPTER 40

"**W**e need to find that painting!" I exclaimed.

Yes. I get stoked whenever someone mentions a new treasure in need of hunting.

"Wait a second," said Beck. "How much is the Vermeer worth?"

"Two hundred million," replied Storm.

$200,000,000
PLUS TAX

"Wait a second," said Beck. "Two hundred million? And the Enlightened Ones only want to give us twenty million for finding it?"

"I'm sure we could negotiate the price point," said Ms. Johnston. "*After* we find the painting."

"That Vermeer has been missing for nearly thirty years," said Storm. "What makes you think we can find it?"

"Because we're the Kidds, Storm!" I declared. "Finding stuff that nobody else can find is what we do!"

"When others say stop," added Beck, "we say go."

"Unless we're at a dangerous intersection," I noted.

"True," said Beck. "But, otherwise, we are flat-out treasure-hunting maniacs!

"Chya!" said Tommy. "It's in, like, our DNA."

"And with your amazing brain power," I said, buttering Storm up, "we'll probably find it by this time next week."

Storm nodded. "True. My brain is awesome. Okay. Let's do this thing."

"Bully!" said Uncle Richie, suddenly reinvigo-
rated. "Pamela? Might we impose upon you to fly
us up to Boston first thing in the morning?"

"You don't want to fly up there tonight?" she
asked.

"We all need our rest," said Uncle Richie. "A
night off might restore our bodily vigor for the
quest ahead!"

"A night off sounds like a great idea," said
Tommy, wiggling his eyebrows at Ms. Johnston.
"How about you, me, and a pizza?"

"Tommy?"

"Yeah?"

"Not gonna happen."

Bright and early the next morning, we jetted
from Virginia to Boston. When we disembarked
from the plane, Uncle Richie had a surprise
announcement for Ms. Johnston.

"This is where we bid you adieu, Pamela," he
said.

"Pardon me?" She sounded stunned.

"It means 'so long, farewell, *auf wiedersehen,*
good-bye,'" said Storm.

Ms. Johnston started stammering. "B-b-but..."

"Do not fret," said Uncle Richie. "We will honor our previous financial agreement and provide you with one third of the gross proceeds at the end of this meandering and somewhat convoluted treasure hunt. However, you have not been dealing honestly with us, Pamela. And as Theodore Roosevelt once said, 'Honesty first; then courage; then brains!'"

"I'm sorry you feel that way, Poppie."

"Well, I feel worse," said Tommy, who had the

sad puppy dog look he usually gets when the loves of his life say "buh-bye."

As for me? I was glad to see Ms. Johnston go. She was a little too cozy with the Enlightened Ones and would probably sell us out to anybody if it meant a bigger slice of the pie for her. And, on this particular treasure hunt, the pie had twenty million bananas in it.

"Let me give you a number to call," said Ms. Johnston.

"Awesome!" said Tommy, perking up.

"It's not mine."

Tommy's face flipped back to sad puppy dog.

"If and when you find the Vermeer, make contact with the Enlightened Ones immediately." She pulled a business card out of her flight suit. "Text this number. They will organize the pick-up of the painting and the delivery of our twenty million dollars."

"You mean your six million, six-hundred-sixty-six-thousand, six-hundred-and-sixty-six dollars, and sixty-six cents," said Storm. "Which, if you behave, we could round up to sixty-seven cents."

Ms. Johnston smiled. It wasn't a very nice one. Reminded me of those snarling beagles we met down in Virginia.

"I'll take that," said Uncle Richie, plucking the business card out of Ms. Johnston's fingertips. "I'm sorry we must part this way, Pamela, but you leave me no choice. We cannot have a paid snoop reporting our every move to the highest bidder. I wish you good luck in all your future endeavors. Good day."

"But, Poppie—"

"I said, 'Good day'!"

Ms. Johnston reluctantly returned to her plane.

"Now then," said Uncle Richie, "I suppose we should go into the terminal and arrange a car rental."

"I'll try," said Tommy. "But I don't know how far I can walk with a broken heart."

"Tut, tut, Thomas," said Uncle Richie. "You'll find another fair maiden, one far worthier of your attentions. Remember: there are plenty of fish in the sea."

"Yeah," I said. "And not all of them are sharks!"

CHAPTER 41

We rented a car.

"Something sporty, like my great-nephew, Thomas, here!" Uncle Richie told the girl behind the counter.

Yes. You guessed it. Tommy had already tail-spun into love again.

"I think she likes me, guys," he told us later, when we all piled (make that *squeezed*) into our sporty Mustang convertible. "She gave us a free map!"

We were all super-happy to see Tommy smiling again (and glad to be rid of Ms. Pamela Johnston).

Storm, who can sound exactly like the lady inside a GPS device, gave us turn-by-turn directions to the Isabella Stewart Gardner Museum—without even consulting the map. (Tommy was hugging it.)

We entered the building, which looked like a Venetian palace from the 1400s (not that I've ever been to Venice in the 1400s). We wandered around a little, with Beck gawking at all the art, and ended up in a beautiful garden courtyard.

"I suggest we initiate our expedition by consulting with the security personnel," said Uncle Richie after we'd seen enough of the art on display.

"Good idea," I said. "Maybe one of the guards was even on duty the night of the burglary."

"Doubtful," said Beck. "That was way back in 1990."

"That's not so long ago," I said.

"Uh, hello?" said Beck. "Do the math. We're talking three decades."

"So? What's three decades?"

"Thirty years!"

Yep. Right there, in the Isabella Stewart Gardner Museum's lush garden courtyard, we erupted into Twin Tirade 2004.

"Three decades?" I scoffed. "That's nothing!"

"Nothing? It's two and a half times our entire lives!"

"Did you do that math in your head?" I screamed. "Do you have a calculator hidden in your hair?"

"No, Bickford. I used my brain. Something you could do if you had one."

"Well, I must say, Rebecca, I am impressed."

"Thank you."

"I divided thirty by twelve and somehow ended up with eighteen."

"Probably because you subtracted instead of dividing."

"Oh. Right. Duh. My bad."

"No biggy."

"We're cool?"

"Totally."

As always, our angry diatribe (Mom's vocabulary word of the week last week) was over almost as soon as it began. However, throwing a loud tantrum in the middle of an art museum is never a great idea.

Unless, of course, you're eager to meet some security guards, which we were. So, in this particular instance, our dumb mistake was genius.

"You kids need to pipe down!" whined this guard who looked to be about the same age as Tommy. It also looked like he'd borrowed his navy-blue blazer from his father, and his baggy gray slacks from Santa Claus. His name tag ID'ed him as Willard.

"Ah, good afternoon, Willard," said Uncle Richie. "I wonder if you might be able to assist us?"

"And I wonder if you can ask these two kids here to pipe down!"

"Of course." He turned to us. "Bick? Beck? Pipe down."

"Yes, sir," we both said.

"Now then, Willard, as I have honored your request, perhaps you will grant me a moment of your time?"

"I'm on the clock, pal. Not supposed to be fraternizing with the art patrons."

"This will take but a moment."

"I ain't got but a moment."

Storm stepped forward, her eyes narrowing and darkening with storm clouds, which, by the way, is how she earned her nickname.

"Then let me make this quick, Willard," she thundered. "What can you tell us about the art theft that took place here in 1990?"

Willard quivered a little.

And then, just like Tommy, he started wiggling

his eyebrows. I think Willard was flirting with Storm.

"I wish I could help you, ma'am," he told her, very earnestly. "More than anything I've ever wished for in my whole, entire life."

Great. Now the security guy was in a tailspin.

"But," he continued, "I wasn't here that night. I wasn't even born. You need to talk to Bob."

"Who's Bob?" asked Storm.

"My boss," said Wilbur. "He's over there in the security office. And, if you ask me, he's the luckiest man in the world."

"Why's that?" asked Storm.

"Because he gets to spend more time with you."

Willard wiggled his eyebrows some more. Storm looked queasy.

But Tommy shot the love-smitten security guard a double thumbs-up. "Smooth moves, Willard. I'm going to borrow that line the next time I rent a car at the Boston airport."

"Thomas?" said Uncle Richie. "We need to move along. We need to visit Bob."

CHAPTER 42

"**A**ya, I was on duty that night," said the security guard named Bob, who was kind of ancient.

If someone stole a painting while he was on duty today, I wouldn't count on Bob to catch the guy. Especially if there was any running involved.

"March eighteenth, nineteen-ninety," he said with a heavy sigh. "Worst day of my life. It was early in the morning. My partner and I buzzed in two police officers responding to a disturbance call. Well, we *thought* they were police officers. Turns out, they were crooks!"

Bob's face turned clown-nose red. He wheezed a little.

"Take it easy," urged Uncle Richie.

"Sorry. Where were we?" He looked around, confused.

"The morning of March eighteenth," said Storm. "Nineteen-ninety."

"That's when the museum was robbed!" shouted Bob, his face going even redder. His head looked like a radish.

"We know," I said.

"Those two thieving robbers tied me and my partner up and spent an hour taking paintings off the walls. Good stuff, too. *The Concert* by Vermeer. Three different Rembrandts! Masterpieces by Manet and Degas. An ancient Chinese gu!"

"They stole some goo?" I said. "And it was Chinese goo?

"Like in moo goo gai pan?" asked Tommy.

"A 'gu' is a ritualistic bronze vessel or vase from the Shang or Zhou dynasties," said Beck.

When it comes to art, my scribbling sibling can out-Storm Storm.

"The museum is offering a five-million-dollar reward for the return of everything," said Bob.

We all nodded. None of us mentioned the fact that the Enlightened Ones were offering us *twenty* million dollars to find just one of the paintings.

"If you find all that art, will you give me a call?" said Bob, handing Uncle Richie a business card with a shiny silver sheriff's star embossed on it. "They're brand-new business cards. A gift

233

from a friend. I feel so bad about what happened. Why, I don't think I've had a decent night's sleep in nearly thirty years."

"Have you tried herbal tea?" suggested Storm.

Bob nodded. "Didn't work. Nothing will work until all that art is safely home here in Boston."

"Is anyone still working the case?" asked Uncle Richie.

"Aya. The FBI's Boston field office. Special Agent Joel McKenna is in charge. He and I talk sometimes. Mostly about natural sleep remedies..."

"Joel McKenna?" said Uncle Richie. "Did he ever work in New York City?"

"Aya," said Bob. "You know him?"

"Indeed, I do. I helped him out on a major case, back in the day. Thank you for your invaluable assistance, Robert."

Apparently, Bob uses his full name on the business cards with the shiny silver star.

We headed out to the parking lot.

"Uncle Richie?" I asked. "Do you really think

an FBI special agent will drop everything he's working on to talk to us?"

"Joel McKenna will. As I said, I helped him close a major case several years ago."

"What kind of case?" asked Tommy.

"An international episode involving kidnapping and ransom."

"Really?" said Beck. "Where?"

Uncle Richie took a moment before he answered. "My portion of the mission took place in Australia, if you must know. The land down under."

"Isn't Australia where you—" Storm blurted before Beck and I cut her off with frantic "zip it, sis" gestures.

You know how the art heist at the Isabella Stewart Gardner Museum was the worst day in Bob the security guard's life?

I have a feeling that whatever happened in Australia (with the fake art objects he had to take back from the museum he'd donated them to) might've been the worst day in Uncle Richie's.

CHAPTER 43

Wе shoehorned ourselves back into the sporty Mustang and headed over to 201 Maple Street in Chelsea, Massachusetts—the FBI field office for all of New England.

We had to stop for visitor badges in the lobby but Special Agent McKenna saw us right away.

"Richie 'Poppie' Luccio!" he said as we stepped into his office. "It is so good to see you again!"

"Likewise, Joel," said Uncle Richie, shaking the crew-cut and buttoned-up agent's hand. "Thank you for agreeing to meet with us on such short notice."

"Happy to help. I still owe you one from that thing down in—"

"Yes," said Uncle Richie.

Wow. He really didn't want anybody talking about whatever happened all those years ago in Australia.

"And you must be the famous Kidd kids—the legendary young treasure hunters! I've worked with your parents in the past. I take it you're Tommy?"

"Chya."

"And you must be Stephanie!"

Storm's eyes started to darken into thunderclouds again.

"We call her Storm, now," said Uncle Richie, quickly.

"Oh," said the special agent. "My apologies."

Storm nodded. "Apology accepted."

"Joel," said Uncle Richie, "you might wonder what brings us to your office today..."

"A totally awesome Mustang," said Tommy. "Got a sweet deal on it at the airport. The counter lady liked me."

"Very true," said Uncle Richie, "but the *reason* we are here is because we would like to chat with you about the nineteen ninety art theft at the Gardner Museum."

"Excellent. It'd be great if the Kidd Family Treasure Hunters could help us find the stolen art."

"We'll do our best, sir," said Storm.

"I have to warn you—this has been one of the most frustrating, baffling, and mysterious cases the FBI has ever dealt with," said the FBI agent. "This file has been open for nearly thirty years."

"Dude?" said Tommy, probably forgetting he was talking to an FBI agent. "We're all about hunting treasures. Especially the ones no one else can find."

"So, what can you tell us?" asked Uncle Richie.

"Not much," said McKenna. "We're pretty certain the art was transported out of New England to either Connecticut or Philadelphia. Maybe both. Stolen property this hot, the thieves would be smart to split it up."

"Totally," says Tommy. "That's what I'd do if I were a thief who stole five hundred million dollars' worth of art, which, hello, I didn't." And then he started sweating. "I wasn't even born in nineteen-ninety. I swear. You want me to take a lie detector test or anything?"

Special Agent McKenna shook his head. "No, thank you, Tommy. That won't be necessary. But, here..." He pulled a bulging binder out of a filing

cabinet. "Take a good look at these pictures. These are the treasures you'll be hunting for."

"Remind me," said Uncle Richie. "What is this smallish painting called? The one with the gentleman in the top hat."

"*Chez Tortoni,*" said Beck, our resident artiste. "It's by Manet."

"And it's worth a lot of Monet!" I quipped. Nobody got the pun, except Uncle Richie.

"Bully, Bick. Bully. Well, thank you, Joel. We won't take up any more of your time. Children? Come along. It's time to go."

"But we just got here," I said.

"And the FBI is quite busy. They have crimes to investigate. We mustn't take up any more of Mr. McKenna's valuable time. Off we go, then."

Uncle Richie hustled us all out the door.

"Quickly, Bick. Put a spring in your step."

"Why the rush?" I asked.

"Because," said Uncle Richie. "I recognized one of those paintings. The Manet that Beck identified for us. I've seen it before."

"Was it a print?" asked Beck.

"No. It was oil on canvas. And, as Beck pointed out, rather small. Perhaps ten by thirteen inches. Most important, it was hanging on the wall in the cards room of a very posh and exclusive private club."

"And why, exactly, is that so important?" asked Storm.

"Because, my dear Storm, that club is in Philadelphia!"

CHAPTER 44

"If we can discover where the folks at the Phinnister Club in Philadelphia obtained that one stolen painting," said Uncle Richie as we raced back to the Boston airport, "we might be able to figure out how to locate the rest of the missing masterpieces!"

"Awesome!" said Tommy.

Uncle Richie purchased plane tickets for all of us. I ended up in the seat next to his.

"This hopping around the country was a lot easier when we had your plane," I said. "Or Ms. Johnston's jet."

"True, Bick. But flying commercial has its advantages, such as free peanuts and pretzels!"

"I just remembered something," I said.

"What's that?"

"You parked your plane at Ms. Johnston's hangar, out there in the desert."

"Indeed, I did."

"But you kind of kicked her off the treasure hunt."

"I thought it best for all concerned."

"Aren't you worried that she'll keep your plane?"

"I suppose it's a possibility. But the stakes in this quest are too high to worry about one antique airplane."

"Well, she'll probably give it back to you, anyway. Right after we give her one third of the Enlightened Ones' twenty-million-dollar finder's fee."

"Bick?"

"Yes, sir?"

"If and when we locate the missing treasures

from the Gardner Museum, we will not be turning them over to these so-called Enlightened Ones."

"We won't?"

He shook his head. "Of course not. These world-class works of art were not meant to hang in some consortium of billionaires' secret and mysterious private collection. No, my good boy, we will return all the stolen objects to the museum in Boston, where art lovers from all over can, once again, see them on display."

I was kind of glad Uncle Richie felt that way.

Treasures like Rembrandts and Manets are meant to be shared, not hoarded.

When we landed in Philadelphia, we took a taxi to the private Phinnister Club where, once again, Uncle Richie had a friend.

"Ah, Poppie!" said a man in a tuxedo, who practically pumped Uncle Richie's arm off when they shook hands. "So good to see you again. Are you looking for a friendly game of cards?"

"Not today, Charles. In fact, I'm actually here on a fact-finding expedition."

"Then how may I be of assistance?"

"We'd like to look at your Manet," said Beck, because she was eager to eyeball the painting up close. Probably so she could count the brush-strokes. She did that sometimes.

"Do we have a Manet?" said Charles.

"It's that small painting of the man in the hat," said Uncle Richie. "In the card room."

"Really? Will wonders never cease? Follow me. And children?"

"Yes, sir?" I said.

IT'S SO SMALL IT REMINDS ME OF A POSTAGE STAMP.

"Don't touch anything."

We were escorted into a very fancy room with a high ceiling, lots of velvety drapes, and a tinkling crystal chandelier. I counted six felt-topped card tables. Only one was occupied. Two elderly gentlemen were grumbling at each other and angrily flipping down cards, playing a very heated game of war.

"There it is!" gushed Beck, pointing to a smallish framed oil painting on the wall.

We rushed over to examine it.

"That looks exactly like the missing Manet!" I said as we crowded around the miniature masterpiece.

"It sure does," said Beck.

Storm whipped out a magnifying glass and handed it to Beck. Yes, she never leaves home without one.

"Notice the loose brushstrokes, simplification of details, and, of course, the suppression of transitional tones," said Beck. "I'd love to do some further tests and scans but, I am ninety percent certain this is the real deal."

247

"Woo-hoo!" said Tommy. "This is why we're the best treasure hunters in the world! Painting's missing for thirty years? Boom! We find it in one day. Who's more awesome than us?"

Uncle Richie turned to his friend Charles.

"Do you know where this painting came from?"

Charles shook his head. "It's just always been there..."

"I know where it came from!" shouted one of the old men flipping cards at the table. "I won it in a game of high-stakes go fish from a lady named Simone Bouffant. It was such a pretty little painting, I decided to donate it to the club."

"Do you know where we might find Ms. Bouffant?" asked Uncle Richie.

"No. Though I wish I did. For she was a fascinating and fetching woman." Then he wiggled his shaggy eyebrows the way Tommy does when he's flirting. I guess it's something guys learn and never forget.

"Miss Bouffant runs an art gallery over near Society Hill," said his card partner. "Fourth and Walnut."

"How do you know that?" snapped the first old man.

"Simone and I dated for a little while!"

"Why, you rascal! We were dating, too!"

They started flinging cards at each other.

"Children?" said Uncle Richie, ducking. "I believe we need to leave here. Immediately."

"Yeah," said Beck. "Let's go find Miss Bouffant before her two boyfriends decapitate us with flying ninja playing cards!"

CHAPTER 45

We grabbed the subway on the Market-Frankford line to the Independence Hall station.

"Might as well take in a few tourist attractions along the way," said Uncle Richie.

"Might as well grab a Philly cheesesteak, too," said Tommy. "And maybe some cream cheese. I'm starving."

"First things first," said Uncle Richie, as we dashed by the Liberty Bell.

"Yep," said Beck, glancing at it as we rushed past. "It's still cracked."

"No time to stop and savor the historical sig-nificance," said Uncle Richie. "I fear one of those two elderly gentlemen in the card room might call Miss Bouffant. Alert her that we are coming. Storm? What can you tell us about Independence Hall?"

We were speed-walking past it.

"Declaration of Independence. US Consti-tution," huffed Storm, giving us the quick bul-let point version of her usual info dump. "Both debated. Signed. Inside."

THIS IS SUPPOSED TO BE THE CITY OF BROTHERLY LOVE. BUT THOSE GUYS BEHIND US DON'T LOOK TOO LOVING.

WHERE'S MY CHEESE STEAK, BRO?

"Bully!" said Uncle Richie. "Kudos on your concise and informative description, Storm."

"Thank you, Uncle Richie."

"Um, you guys?" said Beck, jabbing a thumb over her shoulder. "We're not the only ones racing past Philadelphia's most famous tourist attractions."

I checked behind us.

Dirk McDaniels and three beefy guys in black leather jackets were following us in hot pursuit.

"Those dudes were in the helicopter that followed me when I went to Joshua Tree National Park to dig that fake hole!" said Tommy.

"What are they doing here?" I wondered out loud.

"Following us," said Beck. "Duh."

"I know that!" I snapped back as we all picked up our pace. "But how could they even know we were in Philadelphia?"

"Follow me!" said Uncle Richie.

We ducked into a leafy park across the street

and hid inside a small, Tudor-style maintenance hut.

Thirty seconds later, we saw Dirk McDaniels studying his phone and pointing into the park.

"He's tracking us!" I said. "He's using some kind of app."

"Impossible, little bro," said Tommy. "To do that, one of us would need to be carrying a tracking device."

"One that we brought with us from the desert, to Virginia, to Boston, to Philadelphia," said Storm. "Or picked up somewhere along the way."

Uncle Richie pounded a fist into his open palm. "Bob!"

"Huh?" I said before everybody else could.

Uncle Richie pulled out the business card that the museum security guard had given him. The one with the shiny silver star.

"He said his flashy new cards were a gift from a friend," said Uncle Richie. "I suspect that friend was your parents' archrival Nathan Collier, Mr. McDaniels's boss."

"Collier!" said Tommy, pounding his fist into his palm.

"Of course," said Beck. "He's still trying to beat us to the treasures the Enlightened Ones want."

"Is anyone carrying a crumb of bread?" asked Uncle Richie, peering out the windows of our hiding place in the park.

"I have a sort of half-nibbled protein bar," said Tommy. "It tastes like peanut butter and chalk."

"It might do the trick," said Uncle Richie.

Tommy handed over his crinkled and smooshed bar.

Uncle Richie cracked open the shed door and cooed at some nearby pigeons, sprinkling protein bar crumbs on the ground. The birds pecked their way closer. Uncle Richie scooped up one of the birds, gently petting its feathers, and attached Bob's rolled-up business card to its left leg with a rubber band that he, apparently, kept in his safari vest pocket at all times for just such carrier-pigeon emergencies.

"Fly, my friend, fly!" he urged the bird.

The pigeon took off.

So did Dirk McDaniels and his crew of rough-looking thugs.

"I wonder where that homing pigeon will take them," I said.

Uncle Richie smiled. "Hard to say. But, hopefully, it will be far, far away from Miss Bouffant's art gallery and the answer to the mystery of the missing masterpieces!"

CHAPTER 46

The gallery was closed when we arrived, so we were forced to spend the night at a hotel. Beck said it was a good thing because I was starting to stink more than usual. The next morning we were walking to Walnut Street, when Uncle Richie received an urgent video call from Mom and Dad.

"How's Boston?" asked Mom.

"Actually, Susan," said Uncle Richie, "we're in Philadelphia."

"And I still haven't had a cheesesteak!" said Tommy, dipping in to photobomb the call.

"How ironic," said Dad.

"Tommy's craving for a cheesesteak?" said Uncle Richie.

"No. The fact that you're in Philadelphia, birthplace of the United States Constitution."

"We saw Independence Hall!" I shouted.

"It's still there," added Beck.

"Good to hear," said Dad, with a heavy sigh. "And least some part of this country's historic embrace of freedom isn't under attack."

"What do you mean?" asked Storm.

"Professor Hingleburt has produced yet another long-lost copy of the Bill of Rights. It, too, amends the freedoms we historically know to have been spelled out in the First Amendment."

"What?" I said. "Where'd Hingleburt find it?"

"He didn't," said Mom. "Nathan Collier did."

"Collier!" said Tommy. (And, yes, he pounded his fist into his palm again.)

"How'd he find a missing copy of the Bill of Rights?" I said. "Collier couldn't find a rash at a poison ivy convention!"

"He couldn't find his head with both hands!" added Beck.

It was my turn. "He couldn't find his way out of a paper bag!"

And back to Beck. "He couldn't pour water out of a boot if the instructions were printed on the heel!"

"Be that as it may, Bick and Beck," said Dad, "Collier claims he discovered the long-lost document mounted behind a painting at a garage sale near Schenectady, New York."

"Is the Bill of Rights authentic?" asked Storm.

It was Mom's turn to sigh. "It appears to be. But, again, Dr. Hingleburt is being stingy about access to his discoveries. There are all sorts of tests we'd like to run."

"Wait a second," said Tommy. "How could Nathan Collier find anything in New York when he was out in California chasing us?"

"He has a very large staff," said Mom.

"For sure. One of his main goons, Dirk McDaniels, is actually here in Philly, chasing us around. Well, he was chasing us. Now he's chasing a pigeon."

Mom and Dad looked confused.

"Long story," said Uncle Richie. "But, rest assured, we are all safe, sound, and fit as fiddles. We're following up on a lead related to the infamous Gardner Museum heist in Boston. Once that mission is complete, we shall redirect all our energies to proving that Professor Hingleburt and his bogus Bills of Rights are a sham, a fraud, and an abomination to all that America stands for!"

"As always," said Dad, "we'd welcome any assistance you might be able to offer, Uncle Richie."

"But, frankly, Poppie," said Mom, "there's not much any of us can do. Unless, of course, we can find proof that Dr. Hingleburt is having these very convincing documents counterfeited by a master forger."

We all wished each other good luck and carried on with the tasks at hand.

For us, that meant gaining access to Miss Bouffant's art gallery on Walnut Street.

When we arrived, the door was wide open.

But Miss Bouffant had done a pigeon imitation. She'd flown the coop.

CHAPTER 47

"**T**hose old guys must've called her!" said Tommy, examining the remnants of a half-eaten sandwich sitting on a work table. "The steak on this thing is still warm. The cheese, too. And the roll's kind of soft and squishy..."

"Tommy?" said Storm, shaking her head. "Step away from the half-eaten cheesesteak."

"But..."

"Thomas?" said Uncle Richie. He shook his head, too.

"Fine," said Tommy. "Whatever."

"So, this is super bad luck," said Beck. "Miss Bouffant was our only lead and she vanishes."

261

"Yes, it is, indeed, unfortunate that Miss Bouffant is not here to answer our direct questions," said Uncle Richie, his eyes flitting around the gallery, taking in the artwork. Most of it was contemporary. You know—lots of paint splashes and weird geometric shapes.

"We should be back in DC," said Beck. "Helping Mom and Dad."

"Yeah," I said. "This whole expedition has been a waste of time. California, Virginia, Boston, Philadelphia. And nothing to show for it. Sort of like whatever happened down in Australia."

"I beg your pardon?" said Uncle Richie.

"We heard Dr. Hingleburt talking, Uncle Richie," said Beck. "Back in Washington. Outside the bookstore."

I chimed in. "He said you donated a bunch of so-called treasures to a museum in Australia."

"And then," said Beck, "you had to take them all back because they were fakes."

"If only someone would admit the same thing about all these Bills of Rights that Professor Hingleburt keeps finding," said Storm.

"Uncle Richie?" said Tommy, super-seriously. "We like you. We totally do. But are you a true treasure hunter or are you, like, a total phony?"

Uncle Richie grimaced. "I'd always hoped I'd never have to discuss this matter with you kids."

"Why not?" asked Storm.

"I feared you might find it traumatic."

"Hey," said Tommy, "if it's the truth, we can handle it."

"What happened in Australia?" I asked.

Uncle Richie sat down on a very modern-looking chair. Or it could've been a spindly sculpture. Hard to tell.

"Your parents and I thought it best that we keep this secret, well, secret. This all happened thirteen or more years ago. You, Thomas, were, I think, four. And Stephanie—I mean, Storm—was a newborn infant. Your mother and father were only just becoming famous. They'd discovered a pair of sunken ships off the coast of Florida. Everyone assumed they'd struck it rich. They had, of course, but translating treasure into wealth takes time. However, the kidnappers didn't believe them when your parents tried to explain that they didn't have a million dollars immediately on hand for ransom."

"Wait a second," said Tommy. "Who were they trying to ransom?"

"Yeah," I said. "Who got kidnapped?"

Uncle Richie pursed his lips. Considered his answer. "Thomas and Stephanie."

"No way!" said Tommy. "I don't remember that."

"I'm glad," said Uncle Richie. "The whole ugly episode would be so much worse if you did. That's why we never told you or Storm what happened to you when you were so young. Anyway, Special Agent McKenna was working the kidnapping case for the FBI out of their New York office. Your mother suggested he contact me, to see if I could come up with the money for the ransom. I had just donated a treasure trove to a museum down under. I asked for it back. Pretended that it was all fake and that I was an embarrassing fraud. I then sold the merchandise to the highest bidders and easily raised the ransom money."

"Whoa," said Tommy, sounding stunned.

"That's why Special Agent McKenna owed you a favor," I said.

"And why you called Storm 'Stephanie' when you joined us in DC," added Beck.

Uncle Richie nodded. "The FBI used the ransom money as bait and caught the kidnappers. I could live with the shame of the false story of what happened in Australia—if it meant Tommy and Storm would be home safe and sound."

"You are so cool!" said Beck. Then she, more or less, leaped across the room and hugged

WE LOVE UNCLE RICHIE!

YOU'RE ALSO CRUSHING MY RIBS.

Uncle Richie tight. I joined in. So did Tommy and Storm.

"Uncle Richie?" said Storm when we broke out of our group hug.

"Yes, Storm?"

"You can call me Stephanie anytime you want. You saved our lives."

Uncle Richie grinned. "And I'd do it again. In a heartbeat. But, now, we need to snoop around. There's treasure to be hunted in this art gallery. I can sense it. Spread out, children. Look in every nook and cranny. Try the walls for secret panels, like we did at the Mansion on O Street! This expedition is not over yet!"

We spread out.

We searched the nooks and crannies.

We probed for secret passageways.

We found nothing.

For an hour.

And then, Tommy yawned and leaned against a very white wall.

It swung open.

"You guys?" he called out. "I might have found something."

We all joined him and stepped into a black and empty space where, even though we couldn't see anything, we were bombarded by smells. Turpentine. Canvas. Wood. Glue.

Uncle Richie dug out his phone and fired up the flashlight feature. Its beam swung through the darkness, illuminating a whole lot of nothing.

Until it spot-lit a row of oil paintings stacked against a far wall.

And right there, at the head of the line, was Vermeer's *The Concert.*

The most valuable stolen painting in the world!

CHAPTER 48

"**W**oo-hoo!" I shouted. "The FBI's been searching for this painting for more than thirty years!"

"And we found it in one day!" cried Beck, slapping me a high-five.

"One. Day," said Storm—not sounding nearly as enthusiastic as Beck and me. In fact, she sounded serious. She also had a super-serious look on her face. (There was a lot of squinting and brow-furrowing involved.)

"We should call that FBI dude!" said Tommy. "Collect the reward. Five million bucks is nothing to sneeze at unless, you know, you're allergic to

money, which, hello, I'm totally not."

Beck, our resident art expert, bent down to examine the Vermeer more closely.

"This is so beautiful!" said Beck, admiring the canvas. "Look at those masterful brushstrokes. The purity of light and form conveying a timeless sense of dignity."

"The piano looks pretty cool, too," said Tommy. "But the girl playing it could use a better hairdo."

"Actually, Tommy, that's a harpsichord, not a piano," said Storm.

I looked over at Uncle Richie. He had Storm's serious/pained expression on his face, too. He was also stroking his chin, so Storm started stroking hers. Those two were definitely related.

"You sure we shouldn't do the deal with the Enlightened Ones, Uncle Richie?" said Tommy. "Their reward offer is way bigger..."

"Very sure," mumbled Uncle Richie. I could tell—his mind was somewhere else.

"Hey," I said, "maybe Miss Bouffant has some more of the stolen Boston paintings stashed in here, too!"

"Way to think, little bro!" said Tommy.

He and I started flipping through the line of oil paintings stacked up against one another.

"You guys?" said Beck, who was so excited, she had to fan herself to stop from fainting. "I'm pretty sure this is authentic. This is a real Vermeer!"

"Um, how about this one?" I said.

Because, four paintings down the row of paintings, I'd found another copy of *The Concert*.

"And here's another one of that stolen painting we saw hanging in the card room of the Phinnister Club," said Tommy. "Actually, there's two of 'em. I guess Manet really liked painting that dude with the hat."

"And Vermeer must've had a thing for harpsichords," I added, after finding two more copies of *The Concert*. "Either that, or he had an excellent color copier."

YOU THINK FAMOUS ARTISTS EVER WENT TO KINKO'S OR STAPLES FOR ALL THEIR COPYING NEEDS?

"And that's why we were able to find in one day what the FBI couldn't for more than three decades," said Storm. "These are all forgeries."

"And darn good ones," said Beck. "If you guys hadn't found all those extra copies, I would've sworn that this was a real Vermeer."

"Of course!" said Uncle Richie. "Simone Bouffant must be La Brosse!"

"La Who?" I asked.

"La Brosse. It means, 'the brush.' La Brosse has long been rumored to be the finest, most expert forger to have ever taken up the brush or pen. She could paint Michelangelo's frescoes on your kitchen ceiling and you'd swear you were cooking in the Sistine Chapel."

"And this must be the secret door to her secret studio," said Tommy.

He was at the end of the line of stacked paintings.

They had all been leaning against a small metal doorway, maybe four feet tall and two feet wide.

Those smells of turpentine, wood, and paint? They were even stronger near the hidden doorway.

CHAPTER 49

"Bick? Beck?" said Uncle Richie. "How'd you like to go exploring in La Brosse's secret lair? I believe you two are the only members of our party small enough to squeeze through that doorway."

"We'd love it!" Beck and I said together.

"Bully!" said Uncle Richie. "Did you pack your headlamps?"

"Of course," said Beck.

Beck and I pulled our LED-lamps-on-a-headband devices out of our back pockets and strapped them on.

"This must mean La Brosse is short, too!" said Tommy.

Uncle Richie nodded. "An astute observation, Tommy. 'Short.' We'll keep that description in mind when alerting the authorities."

"Wait a second!" I said. "Do you think Milton T. Mosby, the short guy on the horse who we met down in Virginia, could've been La Brosse in disguise?"

"Doubtful," said Storm. "If La Brosse ever wanted fast cash, she wouldn't need to ride around searching for buried treasure with Civil War reenactors. She'd simply whip up another Rembrandt knockoff."

"True," said Beck. "But Milton T. Mosby is so short..."

"How short is he?" asked Tommy, setting Beck up for a punch line.

"He's so short, he's always the last person to know when it rains."

"Bully for you, Beck!" said Uncle Richie. "Comic relief is always welcome in tense treasure-hunting situations such as these. Now, off you go. Tell us what you find behind that door!"

Beck and I squeezed through the doorway, one at a time.

"And twins?" said Uncle Richie, behind us. "We're counting on you two to help us get to the bottom of this forgery operation!"

"Well," I said, "I guess that means we need to get to the bottom of this spiral staircase, first!"

CHAPTER 50

Beck and I descended the twisting set of narrow steps.

"Careful, you two!" coached Uncle Richie, his voice growing fainter and fainter as Beck and I made our way down the tight spiral staircase. The stinky smell of paint supplies wafted up from down below.

It took us five full minutes to reach the bottom of the stairs, which ended in a dank subterranean vault. We looked around, swinging our headlamp beacons through the darkness. There were paint-splattered easels. A drawing board. Rolls of aged and antique canvas. Mason jars jammed full

of brushes and old-fashioned quill pens.

"What's this?" said Beck, pulling a crinkly tan sheet out of a bin. "It's not canvas."

"You're right. Feels more like parchment. You know, like they would've used for writing the Declaration of—"

Beck looked at me. I looked at her.

Then we looked at those quill pens.

And the parchment.

We both reached the same conclusion at exactly the same split second (it's another twin thing).

"La Brosse also forged those fake Bill of Rights documents!" we shouted.

Our voices echoed under the arches of the low, stone ceiling.

"We need proof!" I said.

"Well, let's look for it," said Beck.

We riffled through stacks of paper and piles of sketchpads and mounds of file folders.

"Look at this!" said Beck, pulling a sheet of paper out of a crisp folder.

It was a printout of an e-mail, with the top part torn off. We couldn't tell who had sent the message to La Brosse, but we could clearly read their instructions:

"Rewrite the First Amendment to read: 'Congress *shall* make laws respecting an establishment of religion, prohibiting the free exercise thereof; abridging the freedom of speech, or of the press; the right of the people peaceably to assemble, and to petition the Government for a redress of grievances.'"

The "shall"—the small but major change to the original "shall not"—was boldfaced and underlined.

There were more instructions: "You will be paid four million dollars. One for each of the four forgeries you will complete for me."

"Do you think Professor Hingleburt is behind this?" I wondered out loud.

"Maybe," said Beck. "But we can't prove it. Unless..."

"La Brosse confesses!" I said, finishing Beck's thought for her.

We knocked knuckles and felt pretty awesome about how clever we were.

Until we both realized something: before "The Brush" could confess, we had to find her!

CHAPTER 51

Beck and I clanked up the spiral of metal steps as quickly as we could, bringing the evidence with us.

"We're pretty sure that La Brosse is the forger behind these fake Bill of Rights that Professor Hingleburt keeps finding," I said, showing Tommy, Storm, and Uncle Richie the sheet of parchment we'd found down in the basement art studio. "And this is probably the quill pen she used to do it!"

"And check this out," said Beck, opening up the file with the incriminating e-mail. "Word-for-word instructions on what the revised First Amendment should say."

Storm scanned the e-mail. "It's an exact match with the wording on all the ones Professor Hingleburt and his associates say they've found."

Uncle Richie clapped Beck and me on our shoulders. "Well done, you two. Well done, indeed!"

"Chya," said Tommy. "You two totally cracked this case wide open."

Storm nodded. "We may not have found the stolen art masterpieces, but we may have uncovered an even more important truth about Professor Hingleburt and his threat to all that America stands for!"

"We need to tell Mom and Dad!" I blurted.

"The sooner the better," said Uncle Richie.

"I've got bars on my phone," said Tommy. "We can video call them now!"

Tommy tapped in Mom's phone number.

She didn't answer.

"That's weird."

So, he tapped in Dad's number.

He didn't answer, either.

"Hmm," said Tommy. "You think they like blocked my number?"

"Try Mom again," I suggested.

Tommy did.

This time, she answered.

"Sorry, Tommy," she said with a whisper. "We really can't talk right now. We're at a lecture. Professor Hingleburt found another 'original' Bill of Rights."

She swung her phone around so we could see Professor Hingleburt standing at the podium in a college lecture hall. The place was packed with

PROFESSOR HINGLEBURT IS TRYING TO TURN
THE BILL OF RIGHTS INTO THE BILL OF WRONGS.
WE NEED TO STOP HIM!

reporters, scholars, and dignified-looking people who were probably senators or cabinet secretaries.

"And so," said Professor Hingleburt, "with the discovery of these four original, authentic, parchment copies of the Bill of Rights, including the one my associate Nathan Collier and his treasure-hunting team retrieved from England just this morning, we must question the legitimacy of the so-called Bill of Rights currently on display at the National Archives. That same list of lies has been published in countless textbooks for two hundred years. Those so-called 'freedoms' are part of a vast, centuries-old conspiracy to warp our founding fathers' original intentions to secure law and order instead of chaos!"

Some people in the audience booed.

Professor Hingleburt grinned. "Oh. I see that the conspiracy to divert America from its true course is still alive and well today here in our nation's capital. Well, boo all you want, ladies and gentlemen. That will not deter me from speaking the truth!"

He waved a document in the air.

"Read the real Bill of Rights. The real one. Freedom was never meant to be the core value of America. Order and discipline and restraint were what the founding fathers had in mind. Long live efficiency and self-control!"

CHAPTER 52

"**W**e need to take whatever evidence we can gather to Washington, immediately!" said Uncle Richie, pointing his finger triumphantly to the ceiling.

He looked like Teddy Roosevelt leading his rough riders up San Juan Hill.

"We have work to do, children. For freedom is not a gift which can be enjoyed save by those who show themselves worthy of it!"

Now he sounded like Teddy Roosevelt, because I'm pretty sure that last bit was a direct quote.

"That was a line from a speech President Theodore Roosevelt made at Gettysburg in 1904," said Storm. (Nailed it.)

"Bully for you, Storm! Abraham Lincoln wasn't the only president to give a Gettysburg Address, where so many died to set men free. But enough with the speechifying—there is work to be done. Bick, Beck? Pack up the parchment, the e-mail, and the quill pen. Tommy and Storm? Roll up a few of those forged paintings."

"You think it will be enough proof to debunk that nutty professor's claims?" I asked.

"I wish we had more, Bick," Uncle Richie said with a sigh. "Some direct link between Hingleburt and La Brosse. But, for now, these items will have to suffice. If we are fortunate, perhaps other evidence shall fall into our hands. But, remember, fortune favors the bold. So, let us boldly go to Washington."

Tommy raised his hand.

"Yes, Tommy?"

"How are we going to get there?"

"The train!" cried Uncle Richie.

"There's an Amtrak Acela Express leaving Philadelphia's 30th Street Station at four eighteen," said Storm, who, I guess, memorizes train schedules in her spare time. "Arriving in Washington's Union Station at six oh four."

"Bully!" cried Uncle Richie. "We need to be on that train."

We packed up all the proof we could—including three copies of the Vermeer—grabbed a cab to the Philadelphia train station, and hopped on the train.

As the Acela Express rumbled south through Wilmington, Delaware and Baltimore, Maryland, my stomach started to rumble.

"I'm kind of hungry," I announced.

"Me, too," said Tommy.

"Well then," said Uncle Richie, "as a refined world traveler, allow me to make a recommendation: the hot dogs in the Amtrak cafe car are some of the finest on the planet. I suggest you accompany them with mustard, relish, and a bag of salty chips." He kissed his thumb and forefinger—the way fancy chefs do. "Magnifique!"

"Sounds great," I said, standing up. "You guys want anything?"

"Bring me one dog with everything on it!" said Uncle Richie.

Storm and Beck weren't interested in hot dogs. But they did get into a conversation about whether a hot dog is a sandwich. (It's one of the greatest unanswerable questions of all time, by the way.)

Tommy and I made our way between cars, moving toward the center of the train where the food car was located. We had to pass through the quiet car (where nobody talked; not even on their phones) and a pair of noisy cars (where everybody talked; especially on their phones).

Finally, we stepped through a whooshing door and entered the cafe car. There was a line at the counter and several people seated on stools at a long bar, eating food out of cardboard containers.

"Hello, Tommy. Bickford."

One of those diners knew who we were.

And we definitely knew who she was, too: trouble!

CHAPTER 53

It was Pamela Johnston!

The lady who ran the airfield out in California, the one Tommy fell in love with, the one who had major league contacts with the Enlightened Ones. The same lady who wanted one third of the E-1's twenty-million-dollar reward for the long-lost Vermeer painting, *The Concert*.

"You found it, didn't you, Tommy?" she said with a flirty smile.

"Maybe," said Tommy.

Tommy was tailspinning again. I could tell. He was wiggling his eyebrows up and down. I think, with him, it's a reflex. Whenever a pretty girl smiles at him, something kicks in and he forgets everything except how to operate his eyebrows.

"And now," Ms. Johnston continued, her voice purring like a contented cat, "you're transporting the...package...down to Washington so your mother can authenticate it. Aren't you?"

"Maybe," said Tommy, trying to lean casually with one hand against the counter so he could look suave and cool. It didn't work. The train was bouncing and so was Tommy.

Ms. Johnston smiled some more. "What a waste of time." She gestured at a skinny man seated next to her. "My friend here, Antoine, is an art expert."

"I am," said Antoine through his nose, which was even skinnier than the rest of his body.

"Antoine would happily authenticate the piece for us."

"I would. Happily."

"What makes you think we found anything?" I asked, trying my best to sound tough.

"I have friends everywhere," said Ms. Johnston. "Including two elderly members of the Phinnister Club in Philadelphia."

"And who are these two dudes?" asked Tommy, gesturing toward Ms. Johnston's other traveling companions. They were muscular and thuggish-looking.

"Oh, they're just friends of my other friends," said Ms. Johnston. "You know: the ones who are very enlightened."

"Only we ain't so enlightened," said one of the goons, cracking and popping his knuckles.

"And we don't know nothin' about art," said the other, cracking and popping his neck.

"But," said Ms. Johnston, "like all of us, they know what they like."

"Oh, yeah?" I said, trying to sound tough. "And what's that?"

Ms. Johnston smiled. "One third of twenty million dollars, of course."

The biggest of the big goons slipped a hand into his jacket, like he was reaching for a concealed weapon.

"Where's the Vermeer, boys?" he sneered. "Time to turn it over to the grown-ups."

I looked to Tommy. "Tommy?"

"Yeah," he said.

And we both took off running.

CHAPTER 54

We dashed through the whooshing glass doors between cars just as the train conductor announced, "Union Station, Washington is our next stop."

"We can lose them in the train station!" I said over my shoulder to Tommy.

"Chya. If they don't catch us on the train first!"

We felt hot air rush up behind us. The two goons had just whooshed through the same sliding doors we did.

Tommy and I danced up the aisle as best we could. The train was rocking and rolling as it rounded curves. We scooted around a big guy hauling his ginormous rolling suitcase out of the overhead bin. He created an excellent blockade!

"Get out of the aisle, pal!" shouted one of the goons when they couldn't get past the man with suitcase.

"I'm getting off at the next stop," said the man.

"Well how about you get out of our way now!" grunted the other goon as he shoved the rolling bag forward. The businessman pushed back. The goons pushed harder. And the next time I looked over my shoulder, the businessman was sitting on top of his suitcase, rolling up the aisle like he was riding in a little red wagon.

Tommy and I barged into the quiet car.

"We need to warn—" Tommy said, before three dozen angry travelers shushed him.

"Sorry," I whispered.

I got shushed, too. I guess even a whisper is too loud for the quiet car.

So, Tommy and I tiptoed as quietly as we could up the aisle. The train started to slow.

"Now arriving Union Station," said the conductor. "Final stop on this train. Union Station."

A door slid open. The two thugs burst into the quiet car. They saw us!

"There they—"

"SHUSH!" said all the quiet car passengers (very loudly).

"Sorry," said one of the goons. Now they were tiptoeing up the aisle, too. Have you ever seen hippos do ballet? It looked like that.

Fortunately, all of the quiet car passengers were getting up out of their seats as the train slowed and we pulled into Union Station. The aisle was crowded with people and suitcases. The two goons were blocked. And they couldn't yell at anybody because, I guess, even goons respect the rules of the quiet car.

Tommy and I made it into the next car.

"We have company," I said to Uncle Richie, Beck, and Storm. "Pamela Johnston and some thugs who work for the Enlightened Ones."

"What does she want?" asked Beck.

"Probably to get back together with me," said Tommy.

"Or the Vermeer," I said. "They know we found something in Philadelphia. Those two old geezers playing war were 'friends' of Ms. Johnston."

"What should we do?" asked Beck.

"Give them the painting," said Storm.

"Huh?" said Beck. "It's a fake."

"Which means we didn't find what the Enlightened Ones were looking for. They will lose interest in us and we'll be able to continue on our true mission unimpeded."

"Does that mean we can do it without anybody messing with us?" asked Tommy.

"Indubitably," said Uncle Richie. "Which, of course, means, 'yes.'"

Tommy nodded. "Cool. Storm? You're a genius."

"Thank you, Tommy."

"Come on," said Uncle Richie. "Let's go give the Enlightened Ones a phony Vermeer so we can also give them the slip!"

CHAPTER 55

We calmly stepped onto the platform at Union Station.

The two goons shoved and tumbled their way out of the quiet car. Ms. Johnston and Antoine, the art appraiser, briskly exited the cafe car.

"Hey, guys!" I said with a wave and a whistle. "We're over here."

The two heavies barreled through the crowd of Amtrak passengers.

"Take it easy," said Storm. "We're not going anywhere."

"Good for you, Storm," said Ms. Johnston as she and her art appraiser hurried over to where we were standing. "I always said you were the smartest member of the Kidd family."

"Well, duh," said Tommy. "Everybody says that. Even me."

"Hello again, Pamela," said Uncle Richie.

She nodded. "Poppie. Oh, I suppose I shouldn't call you that anymore."

"Correct," said Uncle Richie. "But we do have a business agreement. Beck? Would you kindly hand over the Vermeer we discovered in Philadelphia to Ms. Johnston?"

"Sure." Beck unzipped her backpack pulled out a rolled-up tube of canvas.

Ms. Johnston and her art appraiser, Antoine, both looked shocked.

"You carried the most valuable missing painting in the world like...like that?" stammered Ms. Johnston.

Antoine clutched his chest and hyperventilated. "Oh, my..."

"Don't worry," said Beck. "My backpack is waterproof. Here you go."

She tossed the canvas to Ms. Johnston.

Ms. Johnston nearly fainted but snagged the rolled-up tube before it hit the ground.

"Careful, careful," coached Antoine as Ms. Johnston unscrolled the painting. "Let me examine it."

He put on a pair of glasses with weird magnifying lenses as he bent down to inspect the long-missing masterpiece.

"Marvelous," he said. "Simply marvelous. Look

at those masterful brushstrokes. The purity of light and form conveying a timeless sense of dignity."

I looked at Beck. That's exactly what she'd said when she first saw the painting!

Beck just shrugged.

"I am one hundred percent certain that this is the missing Vermeer!" Antoine announced.

"Well done, Richie," said Ms. Johnston. "But since you tried to weasel out of our deal, we're changing that deal."

"You get one third," said the biggest goon. "Pam here gets one half. And we get the other third."

Apparently, math and/or fractions weren't the guy's top talents.

"Fine," said Uncle Richie. "That seems fair."

"Here is your cut," said Ms. Johnston, handing Uncle Richie a gym bag.

He quickly unzipped it. I took a peek. The thing was stuffed with hundred-and thousand-dollar bills.

"Is that six million, six hundred and sixty-six thousand, six hundred and sixty-six dollars?" asked Storm.

"Yes," said Ms. Johnston, handing Storm two

quarters, a dime, a nickel, and a penny. "And here's the missing sixty-six cents."

"You really should've rounded that up to sixty-seven…"

Ms. Johnston smirked. "Maybe next time. Come along, gentlemen. We are expected at a certain top-secret art museum!"

"Is it hidden in a volcano?" I asked. "That's where super villains usually have their lairs…"

Ms. Johnston ignored me and walked away. When she and her cronies were off the platform and in the station, Uncle Richie shook his head.

"This is bad," he said.

"Uh, how so?" said Tommy. "We just got nearly seven million dollars for a phony painting."

"Which we will, of course, donate to charity," said Uncle Richie.

"We will?" I said.

"Ill-gotten gains, Bick. Ill-gotten gains."

"I guess, but…"

Uncle Richie cut me off. "What worries me most is how a world-renowned expert such as this Mr. Antoine, who appraises art for the Enlightened

Ones, could be so easily fooled by La Brosse's masterly technique."

"The lady's good," said Beck. "I thought the Vermeer was real when I first saw it, too."

"Exactly. La Brosse is a master craftsperson. Many will be fooled by her Bill of Rights forgery, too. Many already have been."

"That's why you young whippersnappers need to dig a little deeper!" said an old man in a navy-blue windbreaker and baseball cap.

"Gus?" said Uncle Richie.

"That's right, Poppie. How's your gin rummy game?"

Uncle Richie laughed. "Not much better than the last time you beat me, Gus. Allow me to introduce my great-nieces and -nephews."

"We've already met," said Gus.

"We have?" I said.

"Yes," said Storm, because, don't forget, she has that photographic memory. "You're Gus. The semi-retired park ranger who yelled at us when we were on the lawn surrounding the Washington Monument. I believe you called us 'four young hooligans.'"

"Sorry, about that," said Gus. "But I didn't know who you were."

"But now," said a young woman who'd mysteriously appeared on the platform when we weren't looking, "we do."

It was Rachel.

The park ranger who had given us her business card. The one Tommy kept close to his heart.

CHAPTER 56

We found a hidden room in the basement of Union Station that only Rachel and Gus knew about.

"You guys know all sorts of DC secrets, don't you?" I said, remembering how Rachel's riddle led us to the miniature Washington Monument in the grass surrounding the real deal.

"Yes," said Gus, sounding super-mysterious. "We do."

I heard a high-pitched squeal.

"Sorry," said Gus, adjusting a small hearing aid in his right ear. "Darn thing's new. Have to keep fiddling with the volume or I get feedback.

Can't complain, though. The ear doctor gave it to me for free. Now, where were we?"

"In a secret room hidden deep inside Union Station," said Uncle Richie.

"Right," said Gus. "I knew that."

"We also know that you four Kidds have been on quite an adventure since last we met," said Rachel. She slipped a slim tablet computer out of her park ranger rucksack. She tapped the glass and an animated map filled the illuminated screen. It showed a red dot traveling from Washington to California to Virginia to Boston to

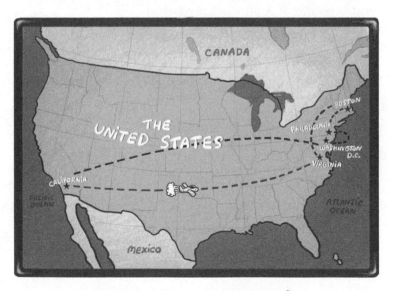

FOLLOW THE BOUNCING KIDDS

Philadelphia and back to Washington.

"You've been tracking us?" said Storm.

"Sorry," said Rachel. "But we had to make certain you were the intrepid treasure hunters we were seeking."

"How'd you do it?" asked Storm.

Rachel held out her hand to Tommy. "Do you still have that business card I gave you when we first met?"

"Chya," said Tommy, pulling out the card with the embossed silver eagle on the front. "I kept it close to my heart at all times. Because falling for you was an extremely short trip."

Yep. His eyebrows were wiggling again.

"That silver eagle is a miniature GPS tracking chip," said Rachel, totally ignoring Tommy's romantic overtures.

"Just like the one Bob gave us in Boston!" said Beck. She turned to the rest of us. "That's it, you guys. From now on, we don't accept any more business cards from anybody if they have shiny silver things stamped on 'em!"

"Deal!" said Tommy.

"Um, you guys don't work for the Enlightened Ones, do you?" I asked. "Because they were sort of testing us, too."

"No," said Gus. "We represent another secret society with a longer and more honorable reputation. The Guardians of Liberty!"

"We're like the Knights Templar who guarded the Holy Grail during the Middle Ages," said Rachel. "I'm the youngest member."

"The prettiest, too," said Tommy. Yep, he was still trying. And his eyebrows were still wiggling up and down like happy caterpillars.

"For centuries," said Gus, "the Guardians of Liberty have protected a secret and extremely secure subterranean chamber filled with our most cherished national treasures. Original copies of all our founding documents. The Declaration of Independence, *The Federalist Papers,* the Constitution, the Bill of Rights..."

"All of them vacuum sealed and protected in thick bulletproof plastic against the elements," added Rachel.

"The original technology was somewhat cruder,

of course, since it was designed by Benjamin Franklin," said Gus. "Through the years, we've made many changes to keep our document-protection facilities the best in the world."

"That must be expensive work," said Uncle Richie.

"It is," said Rachel. "But we get by on donations from generous benefactors."

"Here you go," said Tommy, grabbing the duffel bag stuffed with cash. "From us to you. It's like seven million dollars."

Rachel smiled. "Thank you, Tommy."

"Wait a second," I said. "Why do the Guardians of Liberty need us?"

Rachel looked to Gus.

He nodded.

They were going to tell us everything we needed to know.

CHAPTER 57

"**W**e need you children to help us thwart this diabolical scheme by Professor Hingleburt to rewrite the Bill of Rights!" said Gus, pounding his fist into his palm when he said "Hingle" and "burt."

"Can't you guys just do it?" asked Beck. "Go down to your secret subterranean vault, grab the real deal document, and show the world what a phony Hingleburt is."

Gus shook his head. "No. We can't be publicly involved. We must keep our secret society just that. Secret. Who knows when the next Hingleburtian threat will come? Maybe when young Rachel here is as old as me. No. We need an outside source to discover the documents. Treasure hunters with a world-renowned reputation."

Tommy puffed up his chest a little. "Guess that would be us."

"My reputation isn't all that stellar," said Uncle Richie. "There was an incident in Australia."

Gus nodded. "Where you raised the ransom money for your niece's children."

"You know about that?"

"I have friends at the FBI, too, Poppie. However, you are correct. In the public eye, your reputation is somewhat tainted. That's why we need Tommy, Storm, Beck, and Bick. You four young treasure hunters are quite famous. You must be the ones to 'find' the original copy of the Bill of Rights and bring it out into the daylight to debunk Professor Hingleburt's trumped-up claims."

"And," said Rachel, "we'll show you exactly where it's located!"

"Are you willing to do this for America?" asked Gus. "Because the price of freedom is never free."

"Chya!" said Tommy. "Let's do this thing. USA! USA!"

We piled into a park service van with Rachel behind the wheel.

The sun was starting to set. We were driving toward downtown DC and all the marble buildings and monuments.

"I bet I know where we're going!" I said. "That super-secret bomb shelter vault built in the 1940s underneath the Oliver Wendell Holmes Jr. Memorial. The one we tried to find but everybody, including Rachel here, kept saying it didn't exist."

"It doesn't," said Rachel. "The Guardians of Liberty's current subterranean vault was built in 1848. It replaced the original one Benjamin Franklin dug behind Liberty Hall in Philadelphia, way back in 1777."

"1848?" said Storm. "Isn't that when the Washington Monument was constructed?"

"Exactly," said Gus. "You remember that miniature Washington Monument you children discovered?"

"Sure," I said. "Underneath the manhole cover in the grass."

"It is actually the lock to the vault," said Rachel. "That's why Gus didn't want you touching it."

"But you gave us the riddle that told us how to find it," said Beck.

"We're a team!" snapped Gus. "Rachel gives you the pop quiz. I stop you if you go too far."

"We went too far?" said Storm.

"Almost," said Gus. "You'd have to figure out one more code."

"We can do it!" said Tommy. "Well, Storm probably can."

"She won't need to," said Rachel. She handed Tommy a fresh business card.

"Anything silver stamped on it?" asked Beck.

"Negative," said Tommy. "Just a locker combination. Left to six, right to five, left to two."

"That's how you open the vault," said Gus. "Rotate the pyramid top on the miniature monument, the way you would a dial on a combination lock."

"Then what happens?" asked Uncle Richie.

"The portal will open and you will be able to descend into the vault. Provided, of course, you can fit through the hole." Now the old man smiled at Beck and me. His hearing aid squealed again. "Sorry about that. Where was I?"

"Telling us about the tiny entrance to your tunnel," said Tommy.

"Yes," said Gus. "The entrance is quite narrow. Folks were smaller back in 1848."

"This is another reason we need your help," said Rachel, looking up into the rearview mirror, smiling at Beck and me. "Gus and I are confident that you two will be able to do the job that needs doing."

Yep.

It looked like Beck and I were going to have to squeeze through another secret passageway that nobody else could squeeze through.

CHAPTER 58

We parked as close as we could to the Washington Monument.

"We'll wait here for you," said Gus.

"Good luck," said Rachel.

"Guess I should stay here, too," said Uncle Richie. "You four are on your own. Again."

"Don't worry," said Tommy. "We know how to handle ourselves."

"I know," said Uncle Richie. "Your mother has told me all about your amazing solo adventures— freeing her and finding your father. You four have made me the proudest uncle on the planet. Now, then—off you go. Dare to be great!"

I climbed out of the van with Tommy, Beck, and Storm. We slid the side door shut.

"This way," said Storm, because she, of course, remembered exactly where we had found the miniature monument hidden under the manhole cover.

We scampered across the grass. Fortunately, Gus wasn't there to yell at us to get off George Washington's lawn.

We quickly found the manhole cover and pried off the lid.

Tommy studied the pyramid-shaped top of the miniature monument down in the hole. "I don't see any numbers! How am I supposed to work the combination when I don't know where six, five, and two are?"

"Pretend there's an invisible clock hovering over the tip there," said Beck.

"Okay. Good idea, Beck. But, since the clock is invisible, I still don't see any numbers."

"Pretend the real monument is straight up twelve," coached Beck. "Six would be directly below it, on the opposite side of the hole."

"And five would be close to six," I said. "One

tick up."

"And two would be halfway between one and three, which is halfway down to six!" said Tommy, finally catching on.

"Do it!" I said.

"Hurry," suggested Storm, checking the grounds for security guards. "I suspect that not all of the park rangers are also members of the Guardians of Liberty like Rachel and Gus. They may not be thrilled to see us trespassing on their lawn or fiddling with their secret Washington Monument."

Tommy worked the combination.

Suddenly, the miniature obelisk rose up like a thick, five-foot-tall marble tent pole.

Tommy wrapped his arms around it and yanked it out of its hole.

"It's like a sewer entrance," I said looking down into the open hole. "With ladder rungs running down the side."

"Tommy?" said Storm. "Take that thing to the van! Hurry!"

"Okay." Grunting a little, Tommy jogged off with the heavy stone slab that had to weigh at least two hundred pounds. He's strong that way.

"You guys drop down the hole," said Storm. "I'll slip the cover back on and go wait in the van with Tommy and Uncle Richie."

"Can't you just wait for us to climb back up?" I said.

Storm shook her head. "The park rangers would see me and call the police. You remember how quickly they showed up when Gus caught us that first time."

"How do we get out if you're gone?" asked Beck.

"Just pop the lid open from down below," said Storm. "If you can't, if it's too heavy, just radio us." She tossed me a miniature walkie-talkie because Storm isn't just smart, she's always thinking ahead. "Tommy will come back and pry it open."

Beck and I nodded.

"Sounds like a plan," I said.

"Good luck, you guys," said Storm. "The fate of America as we know it is now in your hands!"

CHAPTER 59

I clipped the miniature walkie-talkie to my web belt and slipped on my headlamp.

Beck slipped hers on, too.

My feet found the rusty iron rungs on the side of the brick-lined well and I started descending into the darkness. Beck's shoes were two rungs above my hands when I heard the wobbly clunk of the manhole cover being dropped back into place.

"You okay?" I asked Beck.

"Yeah. How about you?"

"Never better. It's kind of wild to think about all the other patriots who have climbed down here to protect these cherished documents."

"Yeah," said Beck. "And how short they all were."

We kept working our way down the ladder. Twenty. Thirty. Forty feet.

"This is worse than that spiral staircase at the art gallery," said Beck.

Finally, our feet touched the ground.

"There's some kind of light switch over here," said Beck.

She flicked it up and the lights came on with a *thump* and *thunk* so loud it sounded like someone had just dropped a wobbly steel platter.

"Guess the electrical system is ancient," I said.

"So are those documents!" said Beck, pointing behind me.

I turned around. And there they were, vacuum sealed in a series of thick plastic cases. The documents that created America.

The Declaration of Independence.

The Constitution.

The Bill of Rights.

Beck and I felt compelled to place our hands over our hearts and recite the Pledge of Allegiance.

(It was either that or sing "The Star-Spangled Banner," and nobody wants to hear us try to hit that one high note. We might've shattered the hermetically sealed document holders.)

"Bick?"

"Yeah, Beck?"

"Slight problem."

"What's that?"

"How are we ever going to haul a big, horizontal

case like that up that tunnel we just climbed down?"

It was the old square peg in a round hole conundrum.

"Use the freight elevator!" crackled a tinny voice on my belt.

The walkie-talkie.

"Gus?" I said. "Is that you?"

"Yep."

"Have you been listening to everything we said?"

"We certainly have," said Uncle Richie. "Your recitation of the Pledge was heartfelt and stirring. Bully for you."

"I set the radio up like a baby monitor," said Storm. "Not that you two are babies."

"Gee, thanks, sis," said Beck.

"So, where's this freight elevator?" I asked.

"To the right of the document holders," said Gus. "Can you see it?"

"Yeah. I think so. It looks like two vertical train tracks?"

"Correct," said Gus. "All the document cases

were designed to fit securely between those rails. There are clamps to lock them into place. Then just bop the Launch button."

"Launch?" said Beck.

"Steam-powered hydraulics will propel the document holder upward where it will break through the sod six feet north of the manhole cover."

"I'll be there to snag it!" said Tommy. "I'm good at carrying heavy stuff."

"Excellent," I said. "Come on, Beck. Let's load this rocket launcher."

She and I grabbed hold of the protective plastic case shielding the original copy of the Bill of Rights. We both paused for just a few seconds to admire it and all that it stood for. Then, using every muscle we had, we carried the heavy thing over to the freight elevator, loaded it between the rails, and secured the clamps.

We were all set to bop the Launch button when we were rudely interrupted.

"Not so fast, you two."

We whipped around.

It was Milton T. Mosby. The short guy from Minnesota who'd stolen Mosby's treasure from us in Virginia. That *thunk* we'd heard? It wasn't the electricity coming on. It was Mosby opening the manhole cover!

He had an ornate Civil War pistol.

And it was aimed straight at Beck and me.

CHAPTER 60

"**Y**ou kids aren't taking that document any-where," snarled Mosby.

He was wearing a black cat-burglar outfit, complete with black knit watch cap.

"How'd you know we were down here?" I asked.

"Easy. That old fool Gus who works for the park service? One of our minions posing as an ear doctor fitted him with what he thinks is a free hearing aid. It's actually a highly sophisticated listening device. He and that Rachel girl may think their Guardians of Liberty group is a secret society, but we found out about them a long time ago."

"And who is this 'we'?" asked Beck.

"Never you mind, little girl. Our secret society is super-secret. All you need to know is that we have the money and power to turn America into what it was always meant to be: a place where a select few can live like kings and rule over the rest, turning them into serfs and servants! If we wipe out that First Amendment, we're halfway home to building a new America without all the messy freedoms!"

"Is that why you hired La Brosse to forge those phony Bill of Rights knockoffs?" I asked.

"That's right, little boy. The Brush is the best.

She did an excellent job, right down to the properly aged parchment she scribbled on. She forged those Bill of Rights and made them say exactly what we told her to make them say!"

"How much did you pay Professor Hingleburt to champion your cause?" asked Beck.

"Enough," said Mosby. "But that treasure you dug up for me down in Virginia sure did help us cover some of our expenses! Now, if you don't mind, I'm going to send that very nicely sealed copy of the original Bill of Rights upstairs where

Professor Hingleburt is waiting to receive it. We plan on taking it out of circulation so it doesn't compete with our version of the truth."

"You'll never get away with this!" shouted Beck.

"Oh, really?" sneered Mosby. "Why not?"

"You just totally confessed to us!" I said.

"So? You're just a pair of pesky children. It'd be your word against mine. Nobody listens to children!"

"We'll call the police," shouted Beck.

"Oh, I don't think your cell phones will work this far below ground, little girl."

"We'll call them when we're back outside!"

"Oh, right. I suppose you could do that," said Mosby. "If you were ever going to be outside again."

Beck and I both panicked just a little when he said that.

"What?!?"

"Sorry, kids." Mosby cocked back the hammer on his pistol. "You and your parents have caused Professor Hingleburt and me enough grief. We have other friends standing by topside. They are armed with a welding torch to seal that man-hole cover and a wheelbarrow full of fast-drying cement to cover it up. Once I'm out, you two will be trapped inside this tomb forever." He gestured toward the other documents in their hard-shell cases. "At least you have some excellent reading material to keep you company while you starve to death."

I'd heard enough.

"Well, if you really want this Bill of Rights, guess you better hurry up that ladder."

"What?" said Mosby.

"You don't want somebody else to find it before you do!"

I spun around and bopped the button.

The framed document shot up the freight elevator tracks, fast!

CHAPTER 61

Little Milton Mosby scampered up the side of the well like a squirrel gunning for a bird feeder.

"Don't you two try to follow me!" he hollered. His voice echoed around in the narrow tunnel like an annoying bell.

Then he fired two quick shots behind him.

They rang even louder.

Beck and I gave him a few seconds. Then I ripped the radio off my belt.

"Storm? Tommy? Uncle Richie? Did you guys

hear all that? He confessed! Professor Hingleburt is in on it, too!"

I waited for their reply.

There was none.

"You guys? Hello? He's going to seal us down here like rats in a well!"

Still nothing.

"Great," said Beck. "The batteries must've died in the radio."

"Come on," I said.

"Where are we going?"

"Back up those rusty ladder rungs. He may have quick-drying cement but it can't be *that* quick drying!"

"He'll just lift up the lid and shoot us, Bick!"

"We'll dodge the bullets!"

"What?"

"Hey, Beck—believe you can and you're half-way there!"

Beck rolled her eyes. "Now you sound like Uncle Richie."

"Actually, I think I'm quoting Teddy Roosevelt."

"Same thing," said Beck. "Come on. I'll lead the way."

She dashed over to the ladder.

"You sure you don't want me to go up first?" I asked.

"Yes, Bick. No way do I want to be behind you, your feet, or your farts! Let's go."

We scampered up the ladder. Beck took the lead. I followed. As we neared the top, I heard muffled voices on the other side of the manhole cover.

"Is that Mosby? Do you hear welding?"

"No," said Beck, who was closer to the exit than me.

"How about wet concrete slopping all over the lid? Do you hear that?"

"Nope," said Beck, cheerfully. "All I hear is Tommy and Uncle Richie."

"Huh?"

"They're making some kind of speech."

I heard a metallic *bonk*.

"And guess what?" said Beck. "The manhole cover isn't sealed."

"I've got it," I heard Storm say. Then I heard her grunt.

And I saw light—the white reflection of all those floodlights illuminating the Washington Monument at night.

Beck crawled out of the hole first, of course, but I was right behind her.

And we saw Tommy and Uncle Richie talking to a crowd of people, all of them surrounding Milton Mosby, Professor Hingleburt, a welder, and dude with a wheelbarrow full of gray mud!

"We the people created this country!" said Uncle Richie.

"Totally," added Tommy. He was holding up the Bill of Rights for all to see.

"And," Uncle Richie continued, his voice booming, "we the people will protect our nation and its promise of freedom from all enemies, foreign and domestic—such as these traitors right here!"

"Bully!" cried the crowd. (I figured they must've learned it from Uncle Richie while Beck and I were laddering our way up that tunnel.)

WE HOLD THESE TRUTHS TO BE SELF-EVIDENT: MILTON MOSBY AND PROFESSOR HINGLEBURT ARE PHONIES, FRAUDS, AND TRAITORS!
Bill of Rights
AND THAT THIS FAST-DRYING CONCRETE IS BASICALLY A BOULDER ALREADY...

"I wasn't doing anything except taking an evening stroll," said Mosby, trying to wipe the rust off his hands and the dirt off his pants.

"And I was here doing research," said Professor Hingleburt.

"Actually," said Storm, "you were also making a full and complete confession, Mr. Mosby, in which you implicated Professor Hingleburt in your twisted scheme."

"Ha! I did no such thing!"

"Yes, you did, dude," said Tommy.

"We all heard it," said Gus. "Quite thorough and illuminating."

"And," Storm continued, "thanks to the radio my brave brother Bick was wearing on his belt, we were able to record that confession and immediately turn it over to the FBI."

Gus and Rachel came marching over. They had changed into their park ranger uniforms. They were accompanied by two DC metro police and a troop of folks in FBI windbreakers.

"You're coming with us!" barked Gus, sounding

grumpy. "And you can take back your no-good hearing aid!"

He tossed it at Mosby.

But the little guy couldn't catch it.

Because the police were already cuffing his hands behind his back.

CHAPTER 62

Professor Hingleburt was arrested that night, too.

The welder and construction worker were let go with a warning: "Don't work for sleazy secret-society traitors! They're nefarious and never pay their bills."

La Brosse, the famous forger, slipped away to forge another day.

At Gus and Rachel's request, Beck and I went back down to the deep vault below the Washington Monument to re-install the original copy of the Bill of Rights in its secure location. They sent it back down to us on the freight elevator. Tommy and Storm helped them re-sod the lawn we'd sliced open by sending the document upstairs to reveal the conspiracy against America and its fundamental freedoms.

Professor Hingleburt was unmasked as a phony and a fraud. He was the lead story on every cable news network for three whole days.

Mom and Dad were super-proud of us. And Uncle Richie.

"You always were my favorite uncle," Mom told him at the opening of the Smithsonian exhibit about the lost City of Paititi.

"And you were always my favorite niece, Susan."

They hugged. It was kind of sweet. If you like that sort of mushy stuff.

The exhibit at the Smithsonian was a huge success. All the critics gave it rave reviews. There were lines around the block of ticket holders eager to see the interactive displays and dioramas.

"Our job here is done," said Dad, the next morning over breakfast in our apartment. He sounded satisfied and relieved.

"Do you know what that means?" said Mom, with a sly twinkle in her eye.

"We don't have to stay here in Washington?" I said.

"We can go on another treasure hunt?" added Bick.

"We can do what we were always meant to do?" said Storm. "Explore the world? Go places we've never been before?"

"That's right," Dad said with a laugh.

Tommy sighed. "I guess that means I have to say good-bye to the love of my life."

"Which one?" joked Mom.

Tommy sighed again. "All of them."

"Buck up, Thomas!" said Uncle Richie, bursting into our apartment. "There are new worlds to see and new hearts to conquer. Plus, I brought brekkie in a skillet."

"Huh?" I said.

"Oh, it's a marvelous Melbourne mash-up of eggs and emu sausage. A wonder from the land down under!"

"Australia?" said Beck.

"Right you are, Beck. Have you children ever heard of Lasseter's fabled gold reef?"

"Of course," said Storm. "In 1929 and 1930, Harold Bell Lasseter said he discovered a rich gold deposit in a remote and desolate corner of central Australia."

"But nobody has ever found it," added Dad. "It is the most famous lost mine in all of Australia."

"Yes, indeed," said Uncle Richie. "Why, it almost reminds me of the famous Lost Ship of the Desert, which they said no one could ever find."

"Until we did!" shouted Tommy.

"That's right!"

I turned to Mom and Dad. "You guys? We need to go to Australia!"

"And," said Storm, "Uncle Richie has to come with us!"

Mom and Dad grinned. "Sounds like a plan."

"Bully!" shouted Uncle Richie. "I have a reputation in need of repair in Australia."

"Then let's go repair it!" I said.

"Bully!" shouted everybody else.

Yep. We were all on our way to Australia. And who knows? Maybe Antarctica, too. They were the only two continents we hadn't explored.

And guess what? You get to come with us!

Pack up your pens, Beck. And learn how to draw koala bears and kangaroos!

Look out, Oz. Here come the Kidds!

We're Bick and Beck Kidd, treasure hunters extraordinaire! It's so cool being part of a family that sails around the world, looking for amazing artifacts and being chased by bad guys. You don't want to miss a single one of our epic adventures around the world!
Join us! Read the whole TREASURE HUNTERS SERIES.

JAMES PATTERSON received the Literarian Award for Outstanding Service to the American Literary Community from the National Book Foundation. He holds the Guinness World Record for the most #1 *New York Times* bestsellers, including *Middle School, I Funny,* and *Jacky Ha-Ha,* and his books have sold more than 385 million copies worldwide. A tireless champion of the power of books and reading, Patterson created a children's book imprint, JIMMY Patterson, whose mission is simple: "We want every kid who finishes a JIMMY Book to say, 'PLEASE GIVE ME ANOTHER BOOK.'" He has donated more than one million books to students and soldiers and funds more than four hundred Teacher Education Scholarships at twenty-four colleges and universities. He has also donated millions of dollars to independent bookstores and school libraries. Patterson invests proceeds from the sales of JIMMY Patterson Books in pro-reading initiatives.

CHRIS GRABENSTEIN is a *New York Times* bestselling author who has collaborated with James Patterson on the I Funny, Jacky Ha-Ha, Treasure Hunters, and House of Robots series, as well as *Max Einstein: The Genius Experiment, Word of Mouse, Katt vs. Dogg, Pottymouth and Stoopid, Laugh Out Loud,* and *Daniel X: Armageddon.* He lives in New York City.

JULIANA NEUFELD is an award-winning illustrator who has also worked with James Patterson on the Treasure Hunters and the House of Robots series. Her drawings can be found in books, on album covers, and in nooks and crannies throughout the internet. She lives in Toronto.